Secret Sister

**Other books by Martha Tolles
you might enjoy:**

Darci in Cabin 13
Darci and the Dance Contest
Who's Reading Darci's Diary?
Katie's Baby-sitting Job
Katie and Those Boys
Katie for President
Marrying Off Mom

Secret Sister

Martha Tolles

AN
APPLE
PAPERBACK

SCHOLASTIC INC.
New York Toronto London Auckland Sydney

ISBN 0-590-45245-2

12 11 10 9 8 7 6 5 4 3   3 4 5 6 7/9

Printed in the U.S.A.   28

First Scholastic printing, December 1992

Contents

To my secret admirer, R.

Secret Sister

1.
Crystal

Darci Daniels hurried through the crowded parking lot of Oakwood Middle School, looking for her good friend Jennifer Chen. She had some news and couldn't wait to find her.

She scanned the crowds of boys and girls all around her as they swarmed out of the school buses and on toward the red-brick school building. At last she caught a glimpse of her friend's shiny, dark hair and red jacket bobbing along through the crowd.

"Jennifer, wait. I want to tell you something."

Jennifer whirled around, her glasses glinting in the morning sunlight, and seeing Darci, rushed back to meet her. "Hi, hi." She was smiling, cheerful as usual. "What's up, Darci?"

"I just heard something. We're going to start having secret sisters and brothers."

"Really?" Jennifer's eyes widened behind her glasses. "Sounds great. Who told you?"

1

Darci shifted her shoulder bag excitedly. "I was just talking to the girl I sit with on the bus."

Then the bell rang and the crowds of boys and girls began to surge through the wide double doorway of Oakwood Middle School. "She told me we're going to draw names," Darci went on as they entered the red-brick building, too. "Then we have to write notes to that person, but we can't sign them. That way they'll be anonymous."

"I wonder who we'll get." Jennifer giggled. "And who will get us. I hope it's one of the boys."

"Oh, right." Darci nodded eagerly. "That'd be great." She wouldn't mind drawing a certain boy's name.

When they entered their classroom they saw that their teacher, Miss Jacobs, was already seated at her desk. She was a nice teacher but didn't like them to be noisy, so they just wiggled their fingers good-bye to each other and followed the others to their seats. Darci was so glad she and Jennifer were in the same homeroom together, especially since it was such a big school.

She was also very happy that Nathan was in Miss Jacobs's homeroom. Darci liked Nathan. She thought he liked her, too. She'd just settled into her desk at the front of the room when she saw him come skidding through the doorway just as the second bell rang. With his dark eyes and curly dark hair and a pack slung on his back he looked especially cute this morning, Darci thought. And

2

she almost laughed when he cast a look of mock terror toward Miss Jacobs, then walked down the aisle to his seat.

Smiling, Miss Jacobs stood up a moment later and tapped on her desk. Miss Jacobs wasn't much taller than some of the seventh-grade students and she didn't look much older, either, with her long blonde hair pulled back tightly with a silver clip. "Class, I have something very special I want to discuss with you this morning," Miss Jacobs had said, a pleased look in her blue eyes.

This must be it, Darci thought, the secret brother and sister program. She leaned on her elbows to listen.

"I'm going to pass out names to you," Miss Jacobs went on. "We've mixed them all up with the names from the other seventh-grade rooms."

Oh, too bad, Darci thought. Her chances of picking Nathan's name or his chances of getting hers would be pretty slim.

Just then, the classroom door opened with a swish. There, poised in the doorway, was a small, slender girl with large, dark eyes. She paused for a second, then walked calmly over to Miss Jacobs.

"I'm sorry I'm late," she said, "but I had to do a shoot for a commercial."

A shoot, Darci thought, puzzled for a moment. Then she remembered she'd heard that a new girl, a TV actress, was going to be in their class. She looked like an actress, with that silky black hair

3

pulled off to one side of her head in a long, sleek ponytail and black clips fastened to her ears instead of just regular earrings.

Darci glanced around the room at the others' faces and could see that they were watching, too. Jennifer and Nathan were both eyeing this girl, and Darci, with a sudden dart of worry, hoped that Nathan wasn't too impressed.

"This is Crystal St. Cloud," Miss Jacobs announced to the class. "Crystal, will you have a seat, please?" She motioned toward an empty desk across the aisle and down a few seats from Darci. Crystal walked down the aisle and, as she passed, Darci took a close look at her clothes, a black designer shirt and white pants. A trace of some wonderful perfume lingered on the air, even after she'd gone by. It was probably that Robbie perfume, but Darci couldn't be sure, because she'd had only one sniff of a free sample once in a department store.

Now a wave of whispering swept across the room, and Miss Jacobs spoke firmly. "Class, I'd like your attention again. We have to get on with our discussion. We've got a very exciting plan for this fall. We are going to start something new today.

"Now that we're a few weeks into the school year, the other teachers and I have been talking about how different seventh grade is for you. What with changing classes and being in with so many new boys and girls, you don't have such a

4

good chance to become acquainted with one another. Some of you have been separated from your best friends. Others have come from faraway places — other countries even."

That was true, Darci thought. There was a new girl from India, and a boy from China.

Miss Jacobs went on, her blue eyes shining. "So we've come up with what we think is a great idea. As a means of getting to know one another better, you are going to be asked to draw names and write friendship notes to the boy or girl whose name you have drawn. You will be their secret brothers or sisters for a few weeks, do you see? And someone else will draw your name and write friendly notes to you. Don't forget, the notes must be friendly."

Some of the kids laughed or groaned, but Miss Jacobs just smiled, and from her desk took a box and began to walk up and down the aisles with it. "Boys, take the green papers, and girls, the yellow," she said.

Too bad, Darci thought, now there'd be no chance of drawing Nathan's name.

"Do we all have to do it?" a blonde girl with blue-green eyes asked with a frown. "Maybe we don't want any more friends."

She was a girl named Lisa, someone Darci had had a few problems with last year. Darci was sorry they were in the same room this year.

"Yes, you have to take part, Lisa." Miss Jacobs

5

could be firm. "I'm sure we could all use another friend. Now remember, you are not to tell anyone the name of the person you have drawn. Don't let on in any way, by the expressions on your faces or anything, whose name you've got. Then in a few weeks we will have a friendship party with all the other seventh-graders, and you can reveal your identities."

There was more whispering. "Quiet now," Miss Jacobs warned. But Darci thought the whole idea sounded pretty good, especially for the new students. She remembered how it had been when she'd had to change schools and come here. It would've been great to get friendly notes from someone.

She glanced toward Jennifer, and Jennifer was looking at her, too, and they both rolled their eyes at each other. That meant they were glad they were best friends, but it would also be okay to have some new ones, too. Over the summer their other two best friends had moved away. Some afternoons Jennifer had to take her piano lessons, and some days Darci had to baby-sit her younger brother. So it would be good to have some more friends.

Darci's glance slid over toward Nathan. He was cupping his mouth with his hand and wiggling his fuzzy dark eyebrows while he whispered to the guy behind him. What did he think of all this? Again, with a little twinge of worry, she hoped he wouldn't be too impressed with this new girl, Crystal, with her shiny coil of black hair. For a moment, Darci wished her own wavy brown hair looked like that.

Now Miss Jacobs was coming down Darci's aisle, holding out the box of yellow and green papers. When it was her turn, Darci reached in and took a slip of yellow paper. She opened it and stared in surprise. She'd drawn the name of Crystal! Darci glanced back at her as she bent over her own slip of paper, and felt a little surge of excitement. It could be interesting getting to know her. What was Crystal like anyway? Would she want to be friends with someone who'd never done any acting at all except for being a witch in a fourth-grade play?

Darci began to daydream. Maybe she could invite Crystal over someday — Jennifer, too, of course. They could go up to her room, listen to music, play games, look at her books and photo album. Then she got an even better idea. Maybe she could have a sleepover later on and invite this new girl.

"Have you all got your names now?" Miss Jacobs asked, interrupting Darci's thoughts.

Darci glanced over at Jennifer and waved the yellow paper and smiled. This might really be great. But it would be hard not telling Jennifer whose name she had drawn. Darci scrutinized the others' faces, just in case someone in this room

7

had gotten her name. Was anyone looking at her in some special way? Did Lisa happen to shoot her a quick, unfriendly glance? How Darci hoped Lisa hadn't drawn her name!

The bell rang and everyone stood up and, gathering up books and papers, surged out of the room, heading for the first class. Darci lingered by her desk, watching Crystal as she rose and started up the aisle. She really had stylish clothes, all right, but in a low-key way, not like some of those outrageous outfits Angora and some of the other girls wore, with boots and leather jackets and slicked up hair. Angora was the girl Darci sat with on the bus.

Crystal happened to glance up. "Hi," Darci said. "Hope you like our school."

Crystal smiled. "It looks good so far."

"Where did you move from?" Darci took a few steps toward her.

"We used to live near Hollywood." Crystal let out a little sigh and came over to Darci. "That's a long way from here, isn't it?"

"I know." Darci nodded understandingly. "I used to live in California, too. My name's Darci, by the way." She was pleased they had something in common, pleased Crystal seemed friendly.

They walked toward the door of the classroom together. "It's nice here when you get used to it," Darci went on. "The weather's different from California, of course, but it's pretty when the leaves change color and the snow falls." Darci was just

8

going to add, "Are you going to English class?" She hoped they'd be together. But Lisa and a group of her friends were hovering in the doorway and as Crystal approached they pounced on her.

"Hi," they said, crowding around her. "We've seen a bunch of your ads on TV. My name's Lisa. This is my friend Blythe." Lisa's blue-green eyes were very admiring as she talked to Crystal. "We'd just love to ask you a lot of questions."

They ignored Darci and squeezed her out of the way. They were all buzzing around Crystal like bees around a flower, or maybe it was more like flies around honey.

Just then an eighth-grade boy appeared in the doorway and elbowed his way past the group of girls. He went over to Miss Jacobs and handed her a piece of paper.

"Oh, Darci," Miss Jacobs called out. "Here's a message for you from the office."

Darci, surprised, went up to her. It must be from her mom, but why?

She took the note from Miss Jacobs and read: "Darci, please be sure to come straight home after school. Grandma Clair is coming. Thanks. Mother."

Grandma Clair? How great to see her again. But Darci couldn't help wondering, What was the big rush? Was Grandma Clair coming this very day?

9

2.
Getting Ready

As Darci climbed on the school bus, she kept thinking about the message from her mother. Why was her mother in such a big hurry to have her come home?

She walked down the aisle, looking for the girl she'd been sitting with lately and there she was. "Hi, Angora." Darci flopped into the empty seat Angora had saved for her and smiled gratefully. Today Angora wore a purple leather jacket and as usual had her hair all slicked up high on her head. She also wore a shiny silver medallion on a chain around her neck.

"Angora," Darci exclaimed. "Where did you get that?"

Angora giggled. "A boy. Tony. Isn't it fabulous?"

"Oh, yes, it is." Darci was really impressed. A boy at camp last summer had given her a bracelet, but it kept slipping off her arm. Besides, her friends at camp were all so far away now.

"Do you want to see it?" Angora said to the girls sitting in front of her.

While they were all admiring it, Darci looked out the bus window and thought about her mother's note again. She frowned, worrying, as the bus rattled past a market and a row of shops, then a long street of brown and white houses.

Suddenly, like a dark shadow crossing a sunny field, she remembered a conversation her mother had had with her dad just the other day. "If Mother should visit one of these days," her mother had said, "don't you think she should stay for a good long time?"

"Sure, you bet," her dad had agreed. Her dad was usually ready to go along with most of her mother's ideas. But thinking of this conversation now gave Darci an uneasy feeling. Because how would that work out? Where would Grandma Clair sleep?

Her visits were a lot of fun, of course. She loved to read out loud to Darci and her brothers, Rick and Donny, and she liked to hear all about what they were doing at school and so on, and she also liked to play Scrabble. And it must be good for Grandma Clair to come visit here. She'd retired last year and probably she didn't have as much to do now.

Just then the bus screeched to a stop and Angora poked Darci. "Darci, here's Forest Street."

"Oh, yes, thanks." Darci sprang to her feet,

shouldering her backpack, and smiled down at Angora. "See you tomorrow, and congratulations," she added, eyeing the shiny medallion.

"Sure. Thanks." Angora beamed proudly. "I'll save you a seat again."

Darci hurried down Forest Street, passing white houses and trees with yellowing leaves, passing Nathan's house, too, red brick and just two doors away from hers. She wished he'd been on the bus this afternoon, but he was probably at soccer practice. Up in front of her house she half expected to see her mother's van parked at the curb, waiting to take off for the airport at once.

But all she saw was her younger brother, Donny, out on the lawn, idly tossing a ball in the air over and over near the elm tree. That was where the bees had built a nest last spring, a roundish brown pouch fastened to one of the branches.

"Donny, you'd better be careful," she warned as she turned up the front walk. "You might hit that bees' nest, you know."

"Those old bees won't get me." Donny kept throwing the ball. Donny was lonesome, she knew. Ian, Donny's only friend in the neighborhood, was often at an after-school day camp.

"Grandma Clair's coming," Donny called after her.

"I know," she said over her shoulder. She started up the front steps.

12

When Darci opened the front door and stepped inside, she heard her mother's voice talking on the phone. Darci hurried to the den doorway where she saw her mother sitting at the desk, bent over the phone. But at the sound of Darci's footsteps, she glanced up, her eyes, brown like Darci's, troubled. She went on speaking mechanically into the phone. "I'll meet you at the gate, flight number eleven-thirty-four tomorrow at four-twenty P.M. We can't wait to see you." She hung up the receiver and sighed. "Hello, dear. I couldn't reach your grandmother, as usual. She's always out somewhere these days. But at least she *is* coming here tomorrow."

"Oh, good, Mom." Darci dumped her pack on the couch. "It'll be great to see Grandma Clair again. Remember, last time you didn't get to take her to that new museum and go to the theater." Darci wanted to ask where her grandmother would sleep. But wouldn't she sleep in the den the way she always had?

"I know, Darci," her mother agreed. "I hope we can do a few of those things this time, if they aren't too expensive." Darci knew they were saving money these days for Rick's college expenses. And, after that, there would be Darci's college to pay for.

"But, most of all, Grandma Clair needs a chance to get away and do a little thinking," her mother went on. Darci wondered what her grandma

13

needed to think about. Grandma Clair had been the head of a reading center in Boston before she retired.

"Anyway, let's help her have a really good time, okay, dear? I want her to feel free to stay for a long time."

"Sure, Mom, of course." Darci frowned, thinking about her grandmother. "I guess it's not much fun to get old."

"Old? Well, people still have a good time. They don't change much no matter how many years go by." She reached out and gave Darci a quick hug. "How was school, dear?"

"Oh, fine." Darci broke into a big smile. "Guess what? We're going to have secret sisters and brothers." She explained it to her mother. "And I drew the name of a terrific new girl, Crystal St. Cloud. She's a TV actress. But it's a secret, Mom. Don't tell."

"How interesting." Darci's mother smiled, her brown eyes lighting up. "That could be fun for you to know a girl like that."

"Yes, Mom, I think so, too." Darci paused. Now she just had to ask. She glanced toward the couch. "Will Grandma Clair be sleeping here in the den again?"

"No, dear." Darci's mother stopped smiling. "That's the problem. Since she'll be here for quite a while, it won't work out for her to stay in the den. You know we all like to watch television in

14

here at night, and sometimes Dad and I have to work at the desk."

"Then she could take Donny's room," Darci said quickly, suddenly realizing how easily it could be arranged. "He can move in with Rick." Rick was Darci's older brother, a junior in high school this year.

"Now, Darci, you know that wouldn't do. Rick's homework is far too important for him to lose his quiet study place, and their bedtime hours would be different. And it certainly wouldn't work out for Donny to share with Grandma Clair."

"But, Mom," Darci protested, because all of a sudden she just knew what was coming next. "I need my room."

"I'm so sorry, Darci, but I think it would be best if she roomed with you. That's why I wanted you to come right home. This afternoon I would like you to tidy up your room and clear out part of your closet and your dresser for Grandma Clair's clothes."

Darci stared at her mother, aghast. "But, Mom, you know how Grandma Clair is. She is so neat and wants everything right in place. And besides, I have to have my room when I invite my friends over, like when Crystal comes and all. And Grandma Clair won't like it if I leave my stuff around. Besides, my closet and my dresser are all filled up."

"Darci, Darci." Her mother shook her head.

15

"We have to do this, dear. Your grandmother needs to come for a visit."

The front door slammed and Donny came in and stood in the doorway of the den. "When's Grandma coming?" he asked.

"Tomorrow." Darci glared at her brother. "And she's supposed to sleep in my room instead of yours. It'd be so easy for you and Rick to share a room."

"Me? Sleep in Rick's room?" Donny scowled. "I couldn't do that. His snake might get out of his cage and eat up my goldfish."

"Ah-h-h." Darci tossed her head impatiently. "Your goldfish. How dumb." Darci had a green-brown lizard in a cage, which she loved to watch while she did her homework, but she wouldn't be that silly about it.

"So, Darci, please go clear out some space in your room," her mother said firmly. "I'll let you keep some of your things in that big closet in the upstairs hall."

"But it's going to be so hard." Darci broke off. She didn't mean to sound selfish and she loved her grandma of course, but why couldn't her mother see her problem? As for Donny, he was just ridiculous.

"Darci, I know it's going to be difficult in some ways. And I'm so busy, too, since I've taken on my job." Her mother worked part-time now at the *Oakwood News*.

16

"Yes, I know, Mom, and I do want to help."

"Please, go do it then. I must get busy now." Her mother left the den and hurried off toward the kitchen.

Donny spoke up. "What's so bad about Grandma sleeping in your room? I like Grandma. Anyway, you can put your lizard cage in my room if you want."

Darci looked down at her brother's worried face and mussy brown hair and suddenly felt a little sorry she'd been so cross. "I like Grandma, too. You don't understand, Donny. But thanks. That's nice of you. I'll bring my cage in to you."

She went slowly upstairs to her room then, where she sank down on her bed. The other twin bed in her room was piled high with her belongings — books and extra clothes — and her closet was already stuffed full. Darci groaned, looking around. It was a nice room really, with white curtains across the windows and a sloping ceiling, though the flowery wallpaper was faded. She really needed some new paper, but now her chances seemed slimmer than ever.

Darci let out a sigh. How could she invite Crystal and Jennifer and maybe her friend on the bus, Angora, here for a sleepover when she didn't even have her own room? Halloween was coming, too, and that would be such a good time for a sleepover. It'd be great to have a real party, but what could she do now?

17

She stood up with a sigh and went over to her desk for her lizard cage. She'd move that out first, then get to work.

Just as she placed the cage on Donny's bookshelf, the phone rang in the upstairs hall. Darci hurried out of the room to answer it.

"Hi, Darci." It was Jennifer's cheerful voice.

"Oh, Jennifer, you should hear my news. My grandma's coming for a long time and she's going to sleep in my room." Darci couldn't help letting out a little groan.

"Darci, that's too bad," Jennifer sympathized. "I don't mind staying at my grandma's after school." Jennifer had to do that because her mother was away at work. "It'd be hard to room with Grandma, though," she went on. "But look, you can still have people over — why don't you invite Crystal? We always have fun at your house. Why don't we try to sit with her at lunch tomorrow?"

"Okay, let's." Darci felt somewhat better now that they had a plan. "We'll have to act fast. Lisa and her gang are trying to crowd out everyone else."

After they'd finished talking, Darci went back to her room. Another thing she'd do, Darci decided, was write her first friendship note to Crystal. She'd use her best notepaper and write a really nice letter. But first she better clean out her room.

18

She went over to the closet and began to lift out some of her clothes. It was going to be so crowded in here. Then she had a most wonderful thought. Maybe Grandma Clair wouldn't want to share a room with her either. Maybe she'd say, "Just let me have the den as usual." Darci felt comforted by this happy thought.

3.
New Roommate

Late the next afternoon Darci hurried around her room, getting it ready, dusting and polishing. She kept clinging to her one hope though, that Grandma Clair wouldn't want to room with her. Still, Darci knew she couldn't count on this.

Suddenly Darci heard the car pull into the drive out front. She rushed to the window to look out. They were here. Her father was opening the front door of his four-door Chevrolet and helping Grandma Clair out of the car. She was small with wavy gray-brown hair and she looked stylish, as usual, in a slim black coat. She held herself as straight as ever.

Darci's mother followed closely behind them, carrying a bright red tote bag. Darci felt something like a sob catch in her chest. Her grandma. How good to see her. She was ashamed of all her bad thoughts. Darci rushed downstairs to open the front door and meet her.

"Grandma Clair," she cried, flinging her arms

around her grandmother and kissing her soft, wrinkly cheek.

"Darci, oh, darling. It's been a while, hasn't it?" Grandma Clair held her for a long hug. "Let's look at you." She stepped back, inspecting Darci carefully. Darci wished that she'd remembered to tuck in her shirt and brush her hair. But her grandma just smiled and said, "Why, she's prettier than ever." Then she rubbed at Darci's cheek where she'd left a bit of lipstick, her hazel eyes behind her sunglasses still smiling at Darci. "Look how grown-up she is, too."

Darci was pleased by that and smiled gratefully at her grandma.

"Let's go right on upstairs," Darci's mother said busily, heading toward the stairs. "Perhaps we can get you settled before dinner."

"Yes, that's a good idea. I'd like to get my things put away," Grandma agreed, and started briskly up the steps. Grandma was still quite peppy even though she was sixty-five, Darci decided.

"I'll go back out to the car and get her luggage," Darci's dad said behind them.

Up in Darci's room Grandma Clair sank into the low pink armchair near Darci's dresser. She pushed her wavy gray-brown hair off her forehead and glanced around happily. "My, things look quite nice. I guess Darci's learned to be more tidy."

Darci felt a little hurt, a little cross, too. She

21

wasn't all that messy, was she? Besides, her room really did look good, in spite of the old wallpaper.

"Yes, she's worked hard on her room," her mother agreed, shooting Darci a knowing glance, a glance that said, See how well this is going to work out. "And, Mother, we're so glad you're here for a good, long visit."

Darci tried not to feel discouraged at the thought of the long visit. She should remember how hard it must be to be so old, and alone, too. Grandpa had died years ago. Still, she wished her grandmother would say, "Well, now, since it's going to be for quite a while, perhaps some other room arrangement would be better."

And now Grandma wasn't working anymore either. "Do you miss your job, Grandma?" Darci asked. What would Grandma do all the time, she wondered.

Grandma Clair's face took on a serious look. "Well, yes, I do, dear. I loved helping the children learn to read. You remember that boy Robert I told you about? Well, he finally got so he loved stories about animals, and his mother said he was reading every day. Yes, I do miss that." But to Darci's surprise, she broke into a smile. "Now I have other things to do and think about."

From down below, the front door banged and Donny's voice floated up the stairs. "Is Grandma here?" He came pounding up the stairs and stopped at the bedroom door, mussy and sweaty-looking from his soccer game.

But it didn't seem to bother Grandma Clair, who smiled and held open her arms to him. "Donny, darling, hello."

"Hi, hi, Grandma." Donny rushed over to her and let her hug and kiss him.

"Grandma." He pulled away from her. "Do you want to see my room and my goldfish?" He tugged on her hand. "I can read, too. I'll show you." Donny sounded really happy to see her.

"I have a lizard to show you, too, Grandma," Darci put in. "Only he's in Donny's room now." She broke off, knowing she shouldn't explain why.

Darci's mother put her hands on Donny's shoulders. "Why don't you get cleaned up first? Then Grandma can come to your room after a while."

"Donny has a nice room," Darci said quickly, hoping to give Grandma Clair an idea or two. "It's really better than mine."

Her mother shot her a warning glance and just then her dad appeared in the doorway, lugging several suitcases. "Where shall I put these?" he asked.

"Over here, Carl." Darci's mother pointed to Darci's bed. "We'll get them unpacked and out of the way." The bedroom seemed to be getting more crowded and smaller every minute. Wouldn't her grandmother see that?

23

"I can take care of everything," Grandma Clair protested, getting up.

"Well, let us help you at least," Darci's mother said. "Carl, perhaps you could get the card table from the hall closet. We'll set it up in the corner here for extra table space."

Darci's heart sank. Now the bedroom would be really packed full. But of course she went over and helped her mother open the suitcases and lift out clothes and pull out the empty drawers in her dresser. She'd emptied one whole side of the dresser and taken lots of things out of her closet, too. The closet wasn't exactly neat, but she'd stuffed some clothes way in the back and taken others to the hall closet. She must remember to keep her own dresser drawers closed though, because the clothes were in kind of a jumble.

"Well, that will be good to have that extra table space," Grandma Clair said enthusiastically.

"Of course," Darci's mother said. "We want you to have a wonderful time, don't we, Darci?"

"Oh, yes, yes. Sure. Grandma, do you want to play Scrabble later?" That was her grandmother's favorite game. Still, if only her grandma could have a wonderful time and sleep somewhere else, Darci couldn't help wishing. She took another pile of clothes from her mother and put them in a dresser drawer. When was her grandma going to see that this was all too crowded?

"I think a good long breathing spell is just what you need," Darci's mother added in a firm voice.

"Well, I suppose," Grandma Clair said calmly. She picked up a box of stationery, several pens, and a roll of stamps. "This card table will be perfect for my writing paper. I'll be able to write lots of letters." She smiled, looking very pleased.

But Darci's mother frowned. "Yes, well, I know you'll be doing that. But now I'll run down and finish dinner, and Darci, you can stay here and keep Grandma Clair company."

"Okay, Mom." Darci went over to look at the writing paper, white with the address in blue script at the top. It was good for her grandma to have friends to write to while she was here. Why wasn't Mom more pleased about that? Darci remembered that Jennifer's grandma had lost a couple of friends lately, one in a scuba diving accident, another from a heart attack. It was hard to lose friends, Darci knew, even if they'd only moved away. So she was glad her grandma had some.

"Grandma Clair, I'll be writing letters, too. At school we have a new program," and she poured out to her grandma the whole story about Crystal and the secret sisters and brothers. She didn't think she should say anything about wanting to invite Crystal here for a sleepover, though. She just didn't know what to do about that.

All through dinner Darci kept hoping something

25

would happen to make Grandma Clair want to move to another room. But there was just a lot of talk about what everyone was doing and her mother said once again how her grandmother needed time to do some thinking.

"You will do it, won't you, Mother?"

"Yes, yes, of course, Marcia," Grandma Clair said a little impatiently.

"I don't know if you can do much thinking around here," Darci's dad put in with a smile.

"Yeah, it's a zoo," Rick said.

"What's Grandma Clair have to think about?" Darci asked.

"Oh, nothing much," her mother said vaguely. But Darci knew that tone of voice meant there was something.

"We'll talk about it sometime, Darci," her grandma said, smiling kindly at her. Darci guessed she'd have to wait to hear what it was.

After dinner, Grandma Clair went upstairs to see the boys' rooms, and Darci followed. Maybe now her grandmother would get the idea of the boys rooming together.

Rick showed off the vocabulary words he was studying for his PSAT test at school. He'd typed them on cards and hung them on strings across his room.

"Excellent," Grandma Clair murmured approvingly, gazing upwards at the cards. Then she went over and looked at Rick's pet snake, a three-foot-long rosy boa constrictor. His name was Bo and he lay coiled in a glass cage. "He's doing well, isn't he? He hasn't gotten out of his cage again, has he?" Bo had escaped one time.

"No, no," Rick assured her. "He's the greatest."

Then Donny showed her the goldfish in his room and the books in his bookcase he was learning to read. And Grandma admired Darci's lizard, too.

"Wonderful, wonderful," Grandma Clair kept saying. "You have such nice rooms," she said to the boys. "They're neat and tidy and interesting." The boys had had to clean up their rooms, too, before she came. "But I'm the lucky one because I have such a darling roommate." She reached out and patted Darci's arm and Darci felt ashamed.

"Uh, thanks, Grandma," she was just saying when the phone rang.

Darci ran to answer it, glad she didn't have to say whether or not she liked being Grandma's roommate. It might be Jennifer calling.

But when she lifted the receiver she heard a funny, high-sounding voice say, "Hiya, Darci, this is your secret sister."

"My secret sister?" Darci began to smile into the receiver. "Are you kidding?"

"No, no. I really am your secret sister but I have to disguise myself. You know that," the high

27

singsongy voice went on. "You'll hear from me later, though." Click. The phone went dead. Darci burst out laughing. Who was it anyway? Had the voice sounded like anyone she knew? Somehow there was something a little familiar about it, but who could it be? Someone nice, she hoped.

4.
Secret Notes

When Darci first woke up the next morning, she was surprised to hear little noises in her room. Then she remembered she had a roommate. She rolled over. There was Grandma Clair, already dressed in green pants and blouse, and her bed was made, too.

Darci glanced at the clock and saw that it was late. She threw back the covers and leapt out of bed. "Hi, Grandma. I have to hurry. I can't be late to school today because I want to leave a note on Crystal's desk. And Jennifer and I are going to try to get Crystal to sit with us at lunch, too."

"Sounds like a busy day." Grandma Clair smiled. "It's fun to be a secret friend, isn't it? Did you figure out yet who called you last night?"

Darci had told Grandma all about her phone call. "No." Darci shook her head as she headed for her dresser. "But I hope she sends me a note today." Darci smiled. "She was so funny-sounding."

Without thinking what she was doing, Darci

reached down and pulled out a dresser drawer. Grandma Clair looked straight into it. She frowned.

"Oh, my, Darci. I think you need to straighten out your socks. They're all tumbled in there, every which way." She picked up a few. "Some not in pairs, some with holes."

"Yes, I know, Grandma. I've been meaning to do that." Darci hoped it sounded as if that was the only messy drawer she had. She'd have to remember to keep her other dresser drawers closed when her grandma was around. No way she could be as tidy as her grandmother. It was not going to be easy rooming together.

Maybe her grandma sensed what she was thinking because she said, "We had such a good time last night reading *Jane Eyre*, didn't we?"

"Oh, yes, it was great. I love the book so far." It had been cozy, just the two of them tucked in their beds reading about the sad world of Jane. So, of course there were a lot of good things about having Grandma Clair here.

But now it was time to get off to school. She could hardly wait to put her note on Crystal's desk — and ask Crystal if they could eat lunch together.

At school Darci dashed into the building early without even waiting for Jennifer's bus to arrive, then hung around in the hall by her homeroom until Miss Jacobs came along and unlocked the door.

30

"I just want to deliver a note to my secret sister," Darci explained. "I know which is her desk."

Miss Jacobs looked pleased. "Good, Darci. Glad you're getting right into the spirit of our new program." Darci wondered what Miss Jacobs would say if she knew that Darci had gotten a phone call from her secret sister. Anyway, Darci hoped she'd get a note today, too.

She hurried down the aisle to Crystal's desk where she placed the envelope. It was white with green leaves across the top. Quite nice-looking, she thought with satisfaction. Then she hurried back down the hall to her locker.

She took her time stowing her books in it, then, remembering Grandma's complaints about her sock drawer, she tried to stack up a few of her books. But she kept looking over her shoulder, hoping to see Crystal. She was relieved when she saw Lisa walking down the hall alone. At least *she* wasn't talking to Crystal either.

Suddenly the bell rang. Darci jumped up from her locker and joined the crowds of students hurrying to their homerooms.

As she turned into hers, she was surprised to see quite a few boys and girls seated at their desks and already reading friendship notes. But although there were notes on other empty desks, there was no note for her, she saw with a pang of disappointment. Jennifer looked up from her

31

desk, smiling at Darci, and waved a piece of note-book paper. So, lucky Jennifer had gotten one. Nathan had one, too, a really funny letter. It was a roll of white paper. He stood up, unrolled it to the floor, and held it up so everyone could read the large red-crayoned words on it: *"Hello, Nate. You look great. It's just my fate, to draw your name."*

Darci had to laugh. She still wished she could have been the one, whoever he was, to draw Na-than's name. And now she also wished she had come up with a more unusual kind of letter for Crystal.

All around the room, other boys and girls were reading their notes and laughing and showing them off. Miss Jacobs was letting them talk; in fact, she was smiling a lot herself.

Crystal still hadn't come, so Darci sat down and waited impatiently. Lisa had received some stick-ers in an envelope along with her letter, and she handed them around triumphantly to people sit-ting near her. Again, Darci was sorry she hadn't thought of something clever, instead of a plain letter.

But now, here came Crystal, hurrying into the room and slipping into her seat. Darci watched as she picked up the envelope and pulled out the card. As she read it, Darci remembered just what she'd written: *"We all like having you in our school. It's exciting to have such a great-looking TV actress here, and you seem very nice, too. I hope we get to be good friends. I think everyone will want to be friends with you.*"

"Look," Crystal said, handing it to some of the others sitting near her. "I got a really terrific letter." She was smiling.

"That is great," the others agreed. "Pretty stationery, too."

But when it reached Lisa she just shrugged and said, "Not bad. But I got stickers, too."

Then, to Darci's surprise, Crystal brought her letter over to Darci. Darci pretended to read it. "Nice letter," she said, hoping she didn't blush or anything. It was embarrassing to praise her own writing, but at least this gave her a good chance to talk to Crystal.

"Crystal," she said in a low voice, "would you like to sit with us at lunch today, Jennifer and me?" She hoped Lisa didn't hear. She'd probably barge right in and sit with them, too.

"Why, sure." Crystal nodded, swinging the large silver hoops in her ears. "That'd be fun. See you then."

Darci felt triumphant. Lisa and her gang had beaten them to it yesterday, but today Darci vowed things would be different. She might even invite Crystal over to her house. Yes, she might. Now, if she'd only get a secret sister note today, too.

33

5.
Scratch 'n' Sniff

Just as Darci was hurrying down the hall toward her math class, she spotted Jennifer up ahead. "Jennifer." She ran to catch up with her friend. "Guess what? I talked to Crystal. She's going to eat lunch with us."

"Great." Jennifer looked impressed. "Maybe we'll keep Lisa and Blythe from just absolutely taking her over."

"Yes. I was thinking about what you said. Why don't I invite her to my house tomorrow, even if my grandma is there. Could you come then?"

"Oh, yes. I'd love to. I'm supposed to practice my piano lesson, but I think Mom will let me do it later. By the way," Jennifer added, "did you get a note yet from your secret sister?"

Darci made a little face. "No, but I did get a phone call last night from her. And she had such a funny voice. It was the craziest call!"

"She called you?" Jennifer burst out laughing. "How funny. Oh, that's hilarious!"

She bent over, laughing so hard she had to take off her glasses and wipe her eyes. Darci didn't see why it was quite that funny. Suddenly an idea darted into her brain. "Jennifer!" She stared suspiciously at her friend. "It wasn't you, was it?"

"Oh, no, of course not." Jennifer pushed her shiny black hair off her face and looked flustered. "I'd never do that. Don't be silly, Darci." She allowed herself another little laugh. "It's just so funny, that's all." The bell rang for the next class. "We'd better go. See you at lunch, Darci."

Darci kept thinking about all this during science class. It couldn't have been Jennifer who called? Quiet, cheerful, her best friend, Jennifer. No, Darci didn't think so. Jennifer wouldn't do that. It must have been someone else, her real secret sister, whoever that was.

Darci tried to pay attention then to Mr. Frazer, who was discussing insects, the praying mantis in particular, how greedy it was, what harmful insects it ate, and so on. It was interesting enough to make Darci almost forget about her secret sister for a while.

At lunchtime Mr. Frazer asked Darci to erase the blackboard, so of course she'd had to stay and do it. That meant she was late to lunch and, when she came hurrying out of her classroom, there were only a few students still standing around in the hall. There was no sign of Crystal, but she did see Nathan. She headed toward him even though she was in a hurry.

"Hi, Nathan." She smiled at him. "Did you figure out who your secret brother is yet?" She wondered what he thought of all this.

"Ah, well, not yet." He grinned. "Kinda crazy idea, isn't it?"

"Hey, Nathan!" some boys down the hall called to him.

"Have to go. See ya, Darci." Nathan dashed off.

Darci hurried on to the cafeteria to find Jennifer and Crystal. Nathan had so many friends, he probably didn't care one way or the other about secret brothers. She had kind of a sad feeling about him though. He didn't seem to pay much attention to her lately.

Jennifer was waiting for her outside the doorway of the cafeteria. "Have you seen Crystal?" Darci asked anxiously.

"No, I thought I'd better wait for you. I see you were talking to Nathan." Jennifer smiled knowingly.

Darci frowned. "Only for a minute. He had to go off with his friends. He always seems so busy lately."

"Well, he probably is," Jennifer consoled her. "He's always into things, you know. Anyway, let's look for Crystal."

Together they hurried into the large, sunny cafeteria and looked around at all the long tables.

"There she is," Darci said. "I think she's saved seats for us." Darci felt a sudden spark of pleasure.

"Oh, but look who's with her," she added with a groan. "It's Lisa and Blythe again."

"Well, at least we'll be with her, too," Jennifer said. "Let's get our lunch." They rushed over to pick up plates of spaghetti and salad at the food counter and then headed toward Crystal. When Crystal saw them coming, she smiled and waved.

"Hi." Darci smiled back as they reached the table. "Are these seats for us?"

"Yes, of course," Crystal assured her. "I saved them just for you two."

"Oh, thanks. Hi," Darci said to the others. Lisa glanced up, her blue-green eyes cold, and didn't bother to answer. Instead she turned back to Crystal and began to talk again. For someone who'd told Miss Jacobs she didn't want any new friends, Lisa was certainly acting eager for one now, Darci thought.

But in a minute Crystal turned to Darci and Jennifer. "We were just talking about our secret sisters. Of course I have no idea who mine is, but do any of you know?" She took a bite of spaghetti and waited for their answers.

"No, uh-uh." Lisa shrugged. "We got great letters, though. Blythe's letter is on really nice cream-colored stationery."

Darci didn't want to mention that she'd had no

37

letter at all so instead she said, "I had a crazy phone call last night from a girl who said she was my secret sister. She had a high, funny-sounding voice." She began to eat, too, thinking the spaghetti and tomato sauce were pretty good.

"I think a phone call is dumb." Blythe wore her hair in a long braid, which she flipped over her shoulder in a scornful gesture.

"It's not dumb, Blythe," Jennifer spoke firmly. "You're just mad because you didn't get one."

Darci almost smiled. "I don't think it's dumb either," she agreed. Quiet, little Jennifer would stand right up to anybody if she thought it was important. She had stopped being part of Lisa's group last spring because she didn't like the way Lisa was teasing an overweight girl. Darci hadn't liked it either and that's when she and Jennifer became friends.

But now Lisa wasn't looking pleased either. "You really got a phone call?" She sounded envious, too. "Do you think someone was playing a trick on you. What'd she say?"

"Oh, nothing much." But suddenly Darci remembered something about that phone call. "Oh, yes, there was some music in the background though." It might've been piano music. She looked suspiciously at Jennifer. But Jennifer had already said she didn't call.

Jennifer giggled. "Maybe it was one of the girls

in the glee club. They're always singing or playing their tape decks."

"Oh, well, who cares." Lisa turned back to Crystal. "Tell us about making commercials, Crystal." When Lisa spoke to Crystal her voice turned all soft and respectful.

"Well, I've just made one for cat food." Crystal pushed her plate of half-eaten spaghetti out of the way and leaned toward the girls. "Sometimes, if I'm lucky, I get to do an after-school drama, too. I really like that." She told them more about that and then how her mother had to go with her to every filming. "I spend a lot of time with my mom and other grown-ups. Sometimes it's a little too much." She glanced around the cafeteria. "It's great to be here."

Once, while Crystal was talking, Darci glanced around the room and saw Nathan at a table full of boys. He seemed to be looking her way. Again, she hoped he wasn't too impressed with Crystal.

"Do you get paid a lot?" Blythe blurted out.

"Oh, Blythe." Lisa looked cross. Then she leaned forward, obviously waiting for Crystal's answer.

Crystal didn't seem to mind though. "Sometimes I make a lot, especially if they keep running the commercials on TV over and over. I'm saving for my college education."

"I know how that is," Darci put in. "My brother is going to college soon."

39

"How come you had to move here?" Blythe asked Crystal.

Crystal didn't seem to mind the questions. "Oh, my dad got a part in a play here. He's an actor, too." So then they had to know about her dad, and had he been in any movies. No, he hadn't. What play was he in and so on.

All the time they were talking and eating their lunch, Darci had been hoping for a chance to invite Crystal to her house when the others weren't listening. But Lisa and Blythe hung on Crystal's every word.

Then Lisa said, "We have to go talk to our math teacher." She and Blythe pushed back their chairs and stood up. At last, Darci thought. But just as they turned to go, Lisa said, "Oh, by the way, Crystal, I was wondering if you could come over to my house someday." She completely ignored Darci and Jennifer as if they weren't even there. "My room has been redecorated. I'd love to show it to you."

"Yes, you should see it," Blythe bent eagerly toward Crystal. "She's got a four-poster bed, a fluffy white rug, her own TV and VCR, and lots of videos, too."

Darci felt a pang of sadness. Her room didn't look anything like that, no way, and she was lucky if Mom and Dad would let her rent one video on the weekend. Lisa's room must be beautiful.

"Why, thanks a lot," Crystal was saying and

she smiled happily. "We're staying at the Oakwood Apartments and I miss our house back in Hollywood. I'd love to come to your house someday."

Crystal glanced toward Darci and Jennifer as if she expected Lisa to invite them, too. But instead Lisa threw them a smug look as if to say, "Try and beat that," and she and Blythe sauntered off.

Darci thought they were pretty rude, but tried not to feel overwhelmed by the description of Lisa's room. She wasn't ready to give up, not yet. "What a coincidence," she exclaimed to Crystal. "Jennifer and I were just about to ask you the same thing — if you'd like to come over to my house. Maybe tomorrow. What do you think?"

"Why, sure, I'd love to." Crystal flashed them a pleased smile. "It's kind of hard, you know, moving to this school and all. I was taking classes in a trailer right on the studio lot."

"This is a big change for you, isn't it?" Jennifer asked.

"It is." Crystal leaned back and glanced around at the other students. "I think I'll like it."

Jennifer leaned confidentially toward Crystal. "We hope you can come tomorrow. We always have a great time over at Darci's."

But that was before Grandma Clair came to visit, Darci thought. Perhaps there was some way

41

she could persuade her grandmother to let them have the bedroom to themselves.

"I'll have to check with my mom, though." Crystal frowned a little. "She keeps my schedule and it's really all filled up sometimes. I'll phone you tonight to let you know."

"Okay. Great." Darci smiled hopefully. "Here's my number." After she'd jotted it down, they all got up from the table and headed out of the cafeteria. Nathan and his group had gone. But the others were still there, watching Darci and Jennifer and Crystal in particular as they crossed the room. Everyone seemed interested in a girl who was a TV actress.

Darci was still thinking about Crystal's possible visit as she twirled the knob on her locker a few minutes later. But when she pulled open the door she saw a white envelope inside. "What's that?" she exclaimed. She picked it up and pulled out a card. It was one of those scratch 'n' sniff cards.

It said: *"Scratch me and sniff,"* and there was a picture of an onion on it. It was signed, *"Your smelly secret sister."* "Smelly?" she exclaimed. At last she'd gotten a note, too. She scratched the picture and there was the faint odor of an onion. "Terrific! How funny." She laughed out loud. Whoever her secret sister was had a real sense of humor. Was this something Jennifer would do? Or one of those girls in the glee club?

"Look!" she called out to a group of girls near her and held out the card.

"Oh-h-h." They all laughed.

And Darci rushed off to show it to others. But she'd watch and see if anyone looked guilty or like someone who might have given it to her.

6.
The Visit

Darci woke up with a feeling of excitement the next morning. Crystal had phoned last night and said she could come over to Darci's house. Jennifer was coming, too, of course. Then, like a dash of cold water, Darci remembered about Grandma Clair. Would there be some way she could ask Grandma Clair to let them have the bedroom to themselves this afternoon?

Darci pulled back the covers and looked around. The room was empty, her grandmother's bed already made as usual. It must be late.

She jumped up and hurriedly pulled up her covers, too. Then she tidied her bedside table and put a stack of paperbacks in her bookcase. Her room looked okay, with its white curtains, and posters up on the walls. But how she wished she had some new wallpaper. Of course that card table over in the corner with her grandmother's belongings on it didn't help. She tried not to think

44

about Lisa's newly redecorated room and four-poster bed, her videos, and all the rest.

Darci dressed quickly in light beige pants with a pale lavender shirt, then leaned toward the mirror to brush her hair. Lavender was good with her brown eyes and hair, she decided, and tried to get the waves in her hair not to stick out the wrong way. Was she pretty? People said she was. She smiled at herself hopefully in the mirror, showing her teeth, which looked white and shiny.

Heading for the door, she threw a last look around her room nervously. Couldn't she and Crystal and Jennifer have a good time here this afternoon? They'd listen to music and look at her new paperbacks and her photo album and she had a great new game they could play.

Darci hurried downstairs to the kitchen. "Hi, everybody." Her family were all seated at the breakfast table — her mom and dad and grandma, Rick and Donny — and they were all reading parts of the morning newspaper, except for Donny.

"You're late," Donny announced, splashing milk into his cereal.

"Good morning, Darci." Dad gave her a quick smile over the edge of his newspaper. "How're things with the secret sisters?"

He'd been at an engineers' meeting last evening, so she hadn't seen him before going to bed. "Oh, great, Dad. Thanks. I got my first note from my secret sister. She must be a lot of fun. She gave me a scratch 'n' sniff note with an onion on it."

Her dad laughed and Grandma Clair said, "It's nice to have a friend writing to you, isn't it?"

"You should know, Mother," Darci's mom said wryly, lowering her section of the newspaper and looking at Grandma.

"But an onion, peeugh," Donny said.

"Oh, Donny," Darci said impatiently. "It's just a joke." She hoped Donny wouldn't make fun of her note or make any trouble this afternoon when her friends came to visit. "Mom, remember I told you last night Crystal and Jennifer are coming over today?"

Mom looked up from her reading. "Yes, dear, I do remember. But I've had a call from the office this morning. They need me there this afternoon for an extra job. Grandma has offered to read to him, but I'm afraid you'll have to help take care of Donny, too."

"Oh, Mom." Darci began to feel cross. "Do I have to baby-sit him?" Donny probably wouldn't want to read all the time. She dreaded having him hanging around, bothering her friends. "Couldn't he go to Ian's house?"

"I'm really sorry, dear, but Ian's mother is away at work today, so you know Ian won't be home."

"And I have a student council meeting." Rick leaned back importantly in his chair. Darci

46

thought he acted like Mr. Big this year, what with all his tests and plans for college. And when he wasn't doing that, he was driving off with his friend Chris in Chris's car to see some girls. Well, Darci had important plans, too.

"I'll be able to entertain Donny," Grandma Clair spoke up, putting down her part of the paper. She looked over at Donny. "We'll read some wonderful stories. Or perhaps we could all do something together," she added with a hopeful glance toward Darci, "like play Scrabble or make some fudge. What do you think?"

Donny had just taken a mouthful, but that didn't stop him from talking. "Good." He sprayed bits of cereal from his mouth. "I really like fudge, Grandma."

But Darci wasn't sure that's what her friends would want to do, spend the afternoon with her grandma and younger brother doing such, well, old-fashioned things. "I don't know, Grandma," she said slowly. How could she say what she really felt? "I sort of thought we'd go up to my room and listen to music and all that."

Fortunately, Rick spoke up then. "So who's your new friend, Darci?"

"Crystal. She's a TV actress. She's in after-school TV movies and commercials, like for cat food." Darci felt proud to have such a friend. "And her father is an actor, too."

Rick raised his eyebrows and even her parents

47

looked impressed. And Grandma Clair said, "A theatrical family. How interesting. I've always loved the theater."

But Donny said, "Who cares?" and dribbled some more cereal out of his mouth. Darci hoped that he wouldn't be eating when her friends were here this afternoon.

In the meantime it was going to be a long day at school. But Darci had fun showing her onion note around to everyone while they were standing in the hall waiting for the bell to ring. Lisa was as bad as Donny though and said, "A note that smells, really."

But everyone else laughed and liked it, Crystal and Jennifer and the boys especially. And Nathan said, "Hey, that's a good one." Lisa didn't criticize it anymore after that. One girl, Margaret, laughed so hard and her face turned so pink, Darci wondered if she was the one who had sent it.

Then, as they were entering their classroom, Crystal drew Darci aside and said, "Darci, I can't wait till this afternoon. My mother says she'd like to give us a ride to your house. Would that be okay with you?"

"Oh, sure." Darci felt pleased about the afternoon already. "Could we take Jennifer, too?"

"Oh, of course. There's plenty of room in my mom's car."

So things were going just fine, though at lunchtime Lisa and Blythe and some others took all the

48

seats near Crystal and they were hanging on her every word and *oh-h-hing* and *ah-h-hing* at everything she said. Darci and Jennifer had to sit at the far end of the table.

"Anyway, we'll be with her this afternoon," Jennifer whispered consolingly. "Besides, we still have each other." Her eyes behind her glasses suddenly looked extra shiny.

"Oh, Jennifer, of course." Darci squeezed her friend's arm. "We'll always be best friends."

"But it would be good if we had a foursome again," Jennifer said. "Who else are you going to invite if you have a sleepover?"

"Well, I was thinking of Angora and then, if we get to know Crystal well enough . . ." Darci let the sentence hang. So much depended on this visit today. She let out a little sigh. "I'm afraid I don't have a room like Lisa's. I suppose a TV actress would have a terrific-looking bedroom, too."

"Don't worry, Darci. It won't matter. We'll find plenty of things to do."

Darci just hoped Jennifer was right.

Anyway, that afternoon they met Crystal out in the parking lot and soon her mother pulled up in a big, light blue Cadillac. Darci felt tense but happy as they climbed into the car.

"This is so nice of you girls to invite Crystal over," Mrs. St. Cloud said as they drove off. She had plump arms and hands and short, dark hair and she wore large, swinging earrings. She

49

seemed pleased Crystal was going visiting. "Crystal misses our yard and home back in Hollywood," Mrs. St. Cloud went on. "It's a big change to get used to living in an apartment."

Still, Darci knew the Oakwood Apartments were very elegant. She'd been there with her mother and remembered the marble floors and mirrored walls. If only her house had just one little marble floor or mirrored wall.

"So have you figured out who your secret sisters are yet?" Mrs. St. Cloud asked over her shoulder.

"We don't know, Mom, but I sure like mine," Crystal said and then, to Darci's utter delight, she added, "She writes me the nicest letters."

"I got a really funny one from mine." Darci told Mrs. St. Cloud about the onion note. "I don't know who on earth she is."

"Maybe it's Margaret," Jennifer said. "She really laughed today at your note. Or say, maybe it's that red-haired girl, you know, the one who's always pulling tricks on people?"

"Hm-m-m, I guess." Darci considered the possibilities. "Too bad they aren't from boys."

Jennifer burst out laughing. "Oh, no way."

And Crystal said, "Wouldn't that be fun? But I'm getting letters from a boy I met back in California. I really like him, too."

"I used to like a boy in California when I lived there," Darci said.

"Then there was one at camp you liked, and

50

now . . ." Jennifer teased her. Darci was too embarrassed to say she liked Nathan, and she noticed Jennifer didn't admit she liked Nathan's friend, Bill, either.

So they kept talking as they drove along, and Darci was hopeful it would be a great afternoon.

But when they pulled up in front of her house, she seemed to see things differently somehow. It was just a white wooden house, not that big, and the lawn out front had a lot of worn brown patches from where they all played. Donny was there now, kicking a ball around, his jacket flung down on the grass.

"Here's where I live," she said. "And that's my brother. My grandma is going to look after him this afternoon," she hastened to add. She didn't want Crystal to think they would have to bother with him.

As they climbed out of the car she called out to Donny, "Where's Grandma?" She almost pointed out to him that Grandma Clair had promised to read to him. Then she decided it was better to leave him outside as long as possible.

"Grandma's in the house," Donny called over his shoulder. He seemed about to say something more, but Darci hurried toward the house with her friends.

"Come on inside," she said to Jennifer and Crystal, opening the front door. She felt that worry again. Did her house look okay, with its old green

51

carpet and beige couch in the living room, the little den with that shaggy brown chair of her dad's, the scratched-up table in the dining room?

She peered into the living room, then the den. "Grandma Clair?" she called, but there was no answer. She looked into the dining room, but it was empty. "Grandma," she called again and hurried back to the kitchen. All was quiet.

"Just a minute," she said to her friends, coming back to the hall. "I'll go look upstairs."

But in the upstairs hall she found her bedroom door was closed. Darci began to get a very ominous feeling. What did this mean? Was Grandma Clair in there? She hurried forward and called out, "Grandma?"

She knocked lightly, then pushed open her door and there on the bed lay her grandmother, with her eyes closed. She was breathing softly in sleep and the pages of a letter lay scattered on the floor beside her. The handwriting on the letter was large and regular.

Darci stared. What was her grandmother doing sleeping like this? Didn't she remember about Darci's visitors this afternoon? Darci peered in for a moment longer but her grandmother's figure on the bed didn't stir. A wave of disappointment swept over Darci. She closed the door and tried to keep back tears as she turned to go back downstairs.

Down below, the front door banged open loudly. "Darci," Donny called.

"Here I am," Darci called, then groaned to herself. She'd have to take care of Donny, too. Why, oh why did things have to turn out like this? Why did Grandma Clair have to take a nap right now? Poor Grandma, was she that tired? And yet, Darci felt cross and upset with her, too. Now how on earth could she and her friends have a good time?

7.
The Bees

Darci hurried down the stairs, cross and worried. How could she entertain Crystal and Jennifer with Grandma Clair asleep in the bedroom?

Darci wished she had thought to get that new game out of her room, but she didn't think she should go back up there now and maybe wake up her grandma. She frowned, thinking about it.

"Hi," she said, walking into the den where Crystal and Jennifer were sitting on the couch, staring at the TV screen. Worse yet, Donny had come inside and was crouched in front of the TV, scowling. It didn't look like the start of a great afternoon. Nothing special, anyway. Darci wished she had a video movie for them to watch at least, but she didn't.

"Hi," she said again, forcing a cheery tone. "Is there something good on?"

"We're watching a talk show," Crystal said. "I always like to see the commercials."

Donny was scowling, which meant he probably wanted to change the program to something else. "It's not very good," he muttered.

Darci decided it would be best to avoid further problems with him. "How'd you like something to eat? Let's go in the kitchen and get a snack," she said to her friends.

As the girls followed her down the hall, she added, "I'm really sorry, but my grandma is taking a nap right now so we can't go up to my room."

"Oh, too bad," Jennifer said sympathetically. She knew that Darci was worried about the afternoon. "My grandma falls asleep on the couch lots of times in the daytime. I guess you do that when you get old."

"Getting old can be hard," Crystal put in. "My grandma had to give up dancing."

"Dancing?" both Darci and Jennifer echoed.

Crystal smiled proudly, "Yes, she's tall and blonde, and she danced in musicals."

"Who-a-a," Darci exclaimed, truly impressed. "How fantastic!"

Darci thought of her little grandma upstairs in bed with her gray-brown hair and her glasses. How exciting to have a grandma who was a dancer! It seemed as if all her grandma wanted to do was read books and write letters.

Out in the kitchen Darci found a bag of chocolate chip cookies in the cupboard. But when she picked it up, she found it was empty. "Too bad," she

55

groaned and crumpled the bag in disappointment. "My brothers must have eaten them."

"That's okay," Jennifer said cheerfully. "Don't worry." What Jennifer really meant was, don't worry about how we can't be up in your bedroom and all the rest of the afternoon, Darci knew.

"Cookies aren't good for us anyway," Crystal said to Darci's relief. "They might make our skin break out." She rubbed her cheek worriedly.

Darci looked at Crystal thoughtfully. "I guess you do have to look your best for your next TV job, don't you?"

"You know it," she groaned. "The cameras and the bright lights show every little defect. I'm supposed to drink a lot of water and eat a lot of vegetables, too."

"That's easy if you eat Chinese food the way we do," Jennifer said with a laugh.

"Good idea. I'll tell my mom. I really want to do well, you know." Crystal got a very determined look on her face. "I have to show my family I can keep up with them. And I might get a job doing a TV ad for See's candy."

Darci was impressed with Crystal's ambition. She got out a bag of apples, and they walked toward the front of the house, munching on them while Crystal told them more about what it was like to be on TV.

"You have to do scenes over and over again,"

56

she explained. "They have to be just right. Besides, I'm also taking drama and dance lessons."

It was really interesting and Darci felt proud all over again to have such a friend.

As they passed the den Darci could see that Donny was still in there scowling and changing the TV programs from channel to channel. It was better to leave him alone. How she wished Grandma Clair would wake up and come downstairs. Darci just couldn't help another surge of annoyance toward her grandmother. Anyway, she had to think of something good to do now.

"Would you like to come upstairs and see my brother's pet snake?" she asked. She could check on her grandmother again while they were up there.

"Snake? A real one? How fabulous." Crystal looked amused.

"He's the greatest. He's a three-foot-long rosy boa constrictor," Jennifer explained. "One time he escaped from his cage. He was found in the weirdest place."

"Oh, no." Crystal laughed. "Tell me more."

While Crystal and Jennifer were in Rick's room, hovering over the snake cage and discussing the time he got out of it and where he was found, Darci hurried to her bedroom.

But the door was still closed and when Darci opened it a crack she saw her grandmother lying on the bed, her gray-brown hair spread out over the pillow. Her breathing was heavy and steady. There was no change.

Darci felt really cross. Why did her grandmother have to sleep all afternoon? Didn't she remember her promise to help with Donny? Though again, she couldn't help feeling sorry for her grandmother for being so old and tired. What could she do now with her friends?

Suddenly, Darci snapped her fingers and had an idea. She hurried back to Rick's room. "Listen, I just thought of something I'd like to show you out on our front lawn."

She led them back downstairs and out the front door. "Come look," she said going over to the foot of the elm tree, where she pointed up dramatically into the yellowing leaves. "See? It's something most people don't have."

There, fastened to one of the branches was a grayish pouch about ten inches long and five inches wide.

"What on earth is it?" Crystal looked puzzled. "I've never seen anything like it."

"It's a bees' nest," Darci said. "Isn't that terrific? The bees built it last spring. Sometimes you can see the bees flying in and out, especially when the bushes out here are blooming in the summer. Bees are so amazing."

Crystal's dark eyes looked worried. "Oh, yes,

58

uh, they are interesting, aren't they?" She took a step backward.

"They are unbelievable," Jennifer added, "the way they gather nectar and make honey out of it."

Crystal was still staring up at the nest when they heard a voice call out, "Hiya, Darci."

Darci whirled around toward the street. There was Nathan, wheeling up on his bike, his curly, dark hair shining in the sunlight.

"Hi, Nathan." Darci smiled. How cute he looked.

"What're you guys doing?" Nathan slid off his bike and sauntered over to them.

At that moment the front door opened and Donny came running out carrying a kickball. "Hi, hi, Nathan. Does anybody want to play kickball? Please, will ya?"

"A little later, Donny," Darci said.

"Yeah, maybe later," Nathan agreed. Then he turned to Crystal. "So you're the TV star?"

"I wouldn't say I was a star exactly," Crystal said modestly. "I've done a few commercials and dramas."

Darci felt that worry again. What if Crystal liked Nathan, and worse yet, what if he liked her? After all, she was nice-looking with that coil of dark, shiny hair and those big, dark eyes. Of course Darci wanted her friends to like this new girl, but not too much, not Nathan.

59

Suddenly Donny kicked his ball up in the air. It hit the tree trunk and bounced off at an upward angle.

"Donny, stop!" Darci shouted, but too late. The ball flew higher and smashed right into the bees' nest. The nest jiggled wildly. After that everything went sort of crazy. A straight line of bees began to pour out of the nest, and everyone started screaming and running around every which way.

"Watch it, watch out," they all yelled.

"Oh, no," Crystal moaned, covering her face.

"Run, quick, get in the house," Darci shrieked. She raced toward the front door and flung it open. She paused to glance back and got a terrible jolt of surprise. Right behind her were Jennifer and Donny. But further back there was Crystal, her hands still over her face, and Nathan had his arm around her and was leading her toward the house.

They all rushed into the house, slamming the door behind them. Inside, Darci leaned against the door for a minute and drew a deep breath. She glanced around the front hall anxiously. "Did any bees get in?" she asked.

Crystal dropped her hands from her face and peered around. "Oh, I hope not. I'd just hate to get a bee sting on my face." She sounded truly worried as she looked around. But at least Nathan had stopped holding her around the waist.

"There's one," Donny yelled suddenly.

60

Sure enough, a bee was gliding up by the light fixture overhead. Nathan ripped off his jacket and whipped it through the air. "Got him," he announced, bending over the fallen bee down on the floor.

"You didn't have to kill it, did you?" Darci asked anxiously.

"Hey, I don't know, maybe not." Nathan peered down at it regretfully.

"I'm really sorry to be so afraid," Crystal apologized. "I had a very bad bee sting last year and my face was all swollen for ages. Maybe you could try to scoop him up and put him outside."

They had just opened the front door a crack to slide the bee out on the step, when a car horn tooted out front. "There's my mom," Crystal said. "I have to go now, but thanks a lot for the afternoon. Do you suppose it's safe to go out?" She laughed nervously.

Darci opened the door further and peeked out. The blue Cadillac was there at the curb but there was no long line of bees anymore. "It looks all clear," she announced.

They all stepped outside, looking around warily. A couple of bees were circling the nest, but that was all.

Darci hoped Nathan wasn't going to put his arm around Crystal again. To her relief he just glanced around and said, "Looks okay now."

"I guess I'll make a run for it." Crystal turned

to Darci. "Thanks for the nice time, Darci. See you guys tomorrow at school." She dashed off to her car, circling the bees' nest as she ran.

" 'Bye. See you," they all called after her. They stood watching her leave as her mother drove off in the blue Cadillac.

"Really nice," Nathan commented. Darci felt sad. Crystal was nice, no doubt about it. But then Nathan added, "And how it shines for such an old one."

"Oh, uh, yes, doesn't it?" Darci agreed eagerly, realizing now he was talking about the Cadillac. "Say, how are you doing with your secret brother and all that?" she added, hoping he would stay for a while.

"Yes, how are things?" Jennifer echoed, smiling at him.

"I have to get going," Nathan said. He obviously wasn't interested in talking about his secret brother, at least not right now. "Besides, there might be another bee attack." With that he turned and hurried across the lawn to his bike. "See ya." He saluted and pedaled off.

" 'Bye, Nathan," Darci called after him. How she wished he'd stayed. She turned to Jennifer with a sigh. "He hardly ever comes over anymore. I just wonder . . ." She broke off, recalling the afternoon's events. "You don't think, well, maybe he likes Crystal?"

To her surprise and relief, Jennifer burst out

62

laughing. "Oh, no, Darci. No way. He was just being polite to her about the bees and all that."

Darci felt a little better about the afternoon after that. Still, it hadn't been the greatest visit in the world. She hoped Crystal had had a good time. An afternoon at Lisa's with her videos and her fancy bedroom and no grandma in it would probably be a lot more exciting.

8.
Secret Meeting

Crystal seemed as friendly as ever after her visit to Darci's and said again what a good time she'd had. Darci hoped she wasn't just being polite and Darci decided to go ahead with her plans for her sleepover.

"Is it okay for me to have one?" She checked with her parents once more as they sat in the den one evening. Grandma Clair was upstairs reading to Donny.

"Yes, of course," Mom said, "but it can't be a large group. As you know, you're sharing your room."

"And she's doing a good job of it, isn't she?" Her dad looked up from a stack of papers on the desk and smiled at her.

"Oh, Dad." Darci tried to feel she deserved the compliment. "It isn't always easy. But thanks, and thanks for letting me have a sleepover. I'll invite my friends tomorrow."

Actually, she had already mentioned it to Angora and Jennifer, of course, so, first thing at school the next day she found Crystal at her locker.

"Hi." She hurried up to her. "Crystal, I'm having a sleepover for Halloween. Do you think you could come?"

"Oh, Darci, how I wish I could." Crystal sounded as if she meant it but she made a sad little face. "But I may have to go to a party with my mom and dad. Could I let you know later?"

"Sure, of course," Darci agreed, hoping Crystal wasn't just trying to think up an excuse. Then she couldn't resist asking, "Have you had any more notes from your secret sister?" How she wished she could tell Crystal that she was the one writing those notes.

"Oh, yes." Crystal smiled, her dark eyes shining. "Another good one this morning."

Darci had to turn her face away to hide a little smile. "That's great," she managed to say. She'd slipped one in Crystal's locker yesterday after school. There'd been stickers on it, too, saying things like *"Terrific," "Top Notch,"* and *"The Greatest."* She wouldn't mind getting another note herself though. It had been days since that scratch 'n' sniff one.

But that very afternoon when Darci came home from school she found a small, white envelope in the mailbox with her name on it. "What's this?" she exclaimed out loud, pausing on the front step.

65

She studied the envelope with interest. It must be from her secret sister.

She ripped it open, pulled out a piece of lined yellow paper. It suddenly flashed through her mind that she'd seen yellow paper like that in Angora's notebook just the other day.

Darci unfolded the letter and began to read: " *'Darci, would you like to find out who I am? Come this afternoon at four o'clock to the apple trees at the corner of your street. I'll be there.'* "

Would she ever! Darci threw back her head and laughed. What a funny person this girl was. Could it possibly be Angora? Maybe it was. She was sort of daring and liked to take chances. She'd be willing to do something like this even though they weren't supposed to tell yet. Miss Jacobs had just announced today, in fact, that the Friendship Party would be later this week. Darci shifted her backpack on her shoulders excitedly and pushed open the front door.

"Hello, I'm home," she called out. At the same time she remembered her mother had said she would be working this afternoon and Donny would be visiting Ian. Darci closed the front door quietly. Maybe Grandma Clair was asleep. But Grandma Clair answered.

"Darci, come on in here."

"Hi, Grandma." There in the den was Grandma Clair, seated on the couch, dressed in a beige pants suit with a bright yellow scarf around her

66

neck. She looked quite stylish. If only Grandma Clair had been down here in the den like this the day Crystal came to visit, Darci couldn't help thinking. Her Grandma had said how sorry she was. "I must have just been worn out from reading and writing so many letters," she'd said apologetically. And now she looked at the bundle of letters Darci was holding. "I see you have some mail there, dear."

"Oh, yes, here it is." Darci held out the stack. She thought some of it was for her grandma, no doubt from her friends back home in Boston.

"I got a letter today, too, Grandma. Look what it says." She held out the piece of yellow paper to her grandmother.

Grandma Clair read it, then smiled up at Darci. "Well, you wouldn't want to miss that meeting, would you? Aren't you dying to know who she is?"

"Yes, I am," Darci confessed. "I have an idea, too. It could be the girl I sit next to on the bus." Darci noticed that Grandma was thumbing through the mail in her lap. "I think you got a letter, also."

Grandma pulled one out. It had that same large, even handwriting on it like the letter Darci remembered seeing the day her grandma fell asleep. Grandma Clair laughed. "I guess I have a secret friend, too."

"Really, Grandma? Why is it a secret?"

"Oh, I was just joking." Grandma Clair glanced

at the clock on the wall. "Isn't it almost time for your meeting?"

But Darci lingered, hating to go off and leave her grandma alone. "I'm glad you've heard from a friend."

"Yes, it's someone I've known for ages. When your grandpa was still alive we used to go hiking with a group of friends up in the mountains of Vermont."

Grandma Clair sounded sad, Darci thought. "Oh, Grandma," she burst out, "It must be hard. Do you miss Grandpa a lot?"

"Yes, always, even though it's been five years now. We were married for a long time, you know, almost forty years — forty happy years." She sighed a little. Then she straightened up a bit and pushed her wavy hair off her forehead. "But one must keep living, keep active. There are lots of things to do, people to know."

"Forty years," Darci echoed. "I wonder what it would be like knowing Nathan for forty years." She laughed, trying to picture Nathan as a man, an old man even. Somehow, she could tell Grandma things she wouldn't tell anyone else.

"Oh, so you like him?" Grandma's eyes were twinkly. "But I heard about a boy at camp last summer?"

"Yes, he was nice, too, but he's far away. Besides, Nathan is always kidding around. I was in a dance contest with him one time, too."

Grandma smiled. "Well, it's good to be friends with a lot of boys. That way, you marry the right one."

Getting married sounded like a long way off to Darci. Besides, she had other things to worry about. She looked at her watch. "I'm afraid I'd better go." She felt another pang of guilt. "Will you be lonesome?"

"No, of course not, dear." Grandma Clair was already looking down at her letter again. "You run along."

"We could play Scrabble when I get back, okay?" Darci promised.

"Yes, dear. Fine." Grandma Clair began to read her letter.

So Darci hurried out of the house and got her bike from the garage and pedaled off down the street. At the corner she parked her bike and flopped down on the ground beneath the apple trees. It was quiet here, shady with small yellow-green leaves hanging overhead like an umbrella. A sweet smell from the ripening apples on the ground drifted up to her. She leaned against a tree trunk and took a deep breath, trying not to feel so excited. Who was this girl who'd sent her the note? Wouldn't it be fun if it was Angora? She'd be just the type to do this sort of thing.

Darci smiled to herself, thinking she'd see Angora come up the street any moment. But all was still on Forest Street.

69

Suddenly she heard voices and there, rounding the corner, came a bunch of boys on their bikes. "Oh, no," Darci groaned. She hoped they wouldn't stop and hang around and maybe scare away Angora or whoever it was. She might not show up if they were here.

But the boys were pedaling fast, all of them talking loudly. They were calling out to one another, "Let's have a game."

"Yeah, at Nathan's."

They stopped in front of Nathan's house and swarmed across his lawn and up to his front door.

Darci got up quickly and moved further back under the trees just to make sure they wouldn't see her. In a minute Nathan came out and they started tossing a football around. Darci thought he looked extra cute, his head flung back as he neatly caught the ball. Again she wondered why he hadn't come over lately — except for that day of the bee attack — or stop to talk to her at school.

She glanced around restlessly. Where was her secret sister anyway?

Darci sat a while longer, restlessly picking up the small, old crab apples and tossing them against the gnarled tree trunks. Though the apples had a good smell to them, they were sour to the taste.

She sighed loudly and scuffed her feet in the clumps of grass. She couldn't wait forever. Where was this girl? Could it be Margaret who'd laughed so hard at the onion note? Or that redhead? She'd asked Darci a lot of questions one day.

Now the boys were swarming off down the street so perhaps her secret sister would show up with them gone. Darci tossed another apple in the air impatiently and waited, but nothing happened. Finally she looked at her watch. She'd been here an hour. That was long enough.

She sprang to her feet, feeling annoyed and hurt, too, and brushed off her clothes, then started down the sidewalk.

She didn't know what to think. Would Angora do this? She wouldn't, not if she could help it anyway. Did someone write that note for a trick and not intend to come? Then Darci had a really terrible thought. If someone not so friendly, like Lisa or Blythe, had gotten her name, this was just the sort of thing they might do.

But look who was coming out of his driveway on his bike and turning up the street this way. Nathan. "Hi," she called out, glad to see him at least.

"Hi, Darci." He pedaled up to her and stopped his bike. "How're things?"

"Oh, okay." Should she tell him about her secret sister not showing up? No, it was too embarrassing. To her great pleasure, he got off his bike and started to wheel it along beside her.

"What happened to your friends?" she asked.

"They went off to the park."

"Aren't you going, too?"

"Oh, yeah, yeah." He paused.

She wondered why he hadn't gone with them. Then she had a terrific idea. Maybe he'd seen her coming down the street and decided to wait for her. She felt so pleased.

"You didn't get any bee stings the other day, did you?"

"No." He laughed. "That was some attack, wasn't it?"

She was just going to ask if he was planning to go to the Friendship Party when, to her disappointment, she saw his friend Bill come around the corner.

"I guess I'd better get going," Nathan said and hopped on his bike. " 'Bye, Darci."

" 'Bye, Nathan." She felt a little better now. At least she'd seen Nathan, even though her secret sister didn't keep the date.

9.
Friendship Party

Darci woke slowly a few days later, seeing as usual the white curtains across her windows, the faded flowery wallpaper and, outside, the yellow leaves on the elm tree. But she had a feeling there was something different about this day.

Then she remembered with a surge of excitement. Today was the Friendship Party. At last she would get to tell Crystal that she, Darci, was her secret sister. And at last she'd find out who hers was, too. She smiled, thinking about the scratch 'n' sniff note and that funny phone call.

But hearing a creaky noise in the room, she rolled over and saw her grandma standing by the dresser in her long print nightgown.

"Good morning, Darci."

Darci threw back the covers and sat up. "Oh, Grandma, it's going to be such a great day."

Grandma Clair smiled at her. "What's happening today?"

Darci jumped out of bed. "We're having our

73

secret sister and brother party at school. At last I'll find out who my secret sister is and why she didn't meet me the other day."

"Well, I'm sure she had a good reason. She would have wanted to, I just know." She smiled fondly at Darci. "And think how pleased Crystal is going to be when she learns that you're her secret sister."

Darci was glad she had confided in her grandma about drawing Crystal's name. It was great to be able to talk to her about it. "Thank you, Grandma." Her grandma was so nice. Darci felt a twinge of guilt and wished she could feel happier about sharing her room.

But now it was time to get ready for the Friendship Party. Darci hurried over to the closet to pull out her favorite outfit, a pale yellow sweater with brown pants. She tried not to open the door so wide Grandma Clair could see inside but she peeked in over Darci's shoulder anyway.

"Oh, my," Grandma Clair said. "What a mess. Someday perhaps I could help you straighten out your things in there."

Darci felt a rush of annoyance and she dreaded the thought of cleaning out her closet. If only Grandma Clair wouldn't look, though of course she knew her grandmother was right. "Oh, all right, Grandma. I was going to clean it out sometime."

"By the way," Grandma Clair went on, "I was wondering if you'd like to go shopping with me in the mall this afternoon. I need to look at dresses and your mother has to work. Would you be too worn out from your party?"

"Oh, no, Grandma. Sure, I could go with you." Darci was eager to make up for her bad feelings about her grandma. And it would be lonesome for her grandma to go shopping by herself. In fact, when Darci thought about Grandma Clair's life, it seemed so empty compared to her own: the party today, all the fun at school, her sleepover, next year, going into eighth grade, and living with her family instead of being all alone.

"Grandma," she burst out. "I hope you don't get too lonesome."

Grandma turned away from brushing her hair in front of the mirror to look at Darci. But to Darci's surprise she didn't look sad, instead she looked quite cheerful.

"Well, I've made up my mind about several things. It's true I miss my work. I really loved helping all those children learn to read. But now . . ." Grandma paused and broke into a smile. "As I told you, there are lots of things to do in life. I think I'll volunteer at the art museum and with the library literacy program and I'll have time to see more of my really special friends."

Darci felt better to hear her grandma was happy about her plans and friends. She knew just how great that was and she could hardly wait for her own plans that afternoon.

75

When the last period of the day came at school, all the seventh-graders headed for the all-purpose room. The room had a festive air. The word *FRIENDSHIP* hung in large colorful letters along one wall and underneath was a big table with pitchers of punch and plates of cookies on it.

Darci and Jennifer hurried into the room and joined the crowd. In a moment Miss Jacobs stood up and started to speak, her blue eyes shining. "All right, everybody," she called out. The other teachers lined up beside her, smiling. "You know whose names you've drawn. So now you, their secret sisters and brothers, may go up to them and make yourselves known."

The crowd began to churn in all directions.

"Let's do it," Darci exclaimed to Jennifer. "But, first, let's tell each other."

"Okay." Jennifer leaned toward her eagerly. "Who's name did you get, Darci?"

Darci laughed. "Oh, you'll never believe it. It's been so hard to keep it from you. It's Crystal."

"Who-o-a-a, Darci." Jennifer let out such a whoop and tossed her head so hard she had to straighten her glasses. "I never guessed. Never." She laughed. "I know she'll be really pleased. She'll definitely come to your sleepover now."

"I hope you're right." Darci glanced around at the crowd. "I'm dying to find out who got my name. I think it must be that redhead. She keeps

76

asking me so many silly questions. But tell me about yours."

"I already know who got my name," Jennifer said. "She just told me out in the hall. It was Julie Kline." Julie Kline was just like Angora, with her leather jacket and boots and slicked back hairdo, the exact opposite of Jennifer. But it didn't matter. Jennifer could get along with anybody.

"And whose name did you draw?" Darci asked Jennifer.

"Oh, uh, uh, a girl named Charlene. She's, uh, moving away. Say, Angora told me she's coming to your sleepover." Jennifer smiled. "Isn't that great?"

"Yes, and if Crystal comes there'll be four of us." Darci was hopeful. Maybe Crystal really had had a good time the day she visited. Maybe she really would want to come again.

Just then Darci spotted Crystal's sleek, dark hair up ahead. "Look, there's Crystal. Let's go catch her." They started off through the crowd. "Oh, Jennifer, won't Crystal be surprised?"

But as they drew closer Darci was disappointed to see that Crystal was not alone. Blythe was with her. Oh, well, it was still going to be fun telling Crystal the news.

"Hi, hi," Darci called out as she and Jennifer approached them. "Oh, Crystal, guess what? I'm your secret sister."

77

"You are, Darci?" Crystal looked astonished. Then she laughed. "How terrific." She threw her arms around Darci and hugged her, then stepped back and looked at Darci with a happy face. "Your letters were wonderful. They really helped me, being in a new school and all. I'm glad it was you." She seemed so pleased, Darci felt warm and happy.

"I'll have to tell Lisa," Blythe said dryly, then turned to Crystal. "I have a message for you from her. She wants to know if you could come to her sleepover on Halloween."

Darci's happiness suddenly evaporated. "Oh, no!"

"Why shouldn't she?" Blythe stared down at Darci haughtily. Blythe was wearing her hair in a long braid down her back. It made her seem taller than ever. "Lisa has a terrific room and she's going to invite a big bunch of boys to stop by, too."

"Well, I . . . I was already planning one and I've invited Crystal," Darci said. "I can't have a very big one," she added. There would be no big bunch of boys either. And her room, well Grandma Clair would be in it, for one thing. It would be hard to compete with Lisa's party.

"Well, that's really nice of you to ask me," Crystal started to say to Blythe.

Just then Lisa came hurrying up to them, apparently through with her friendship act. "Hi,

78

Crystal," she called out, her blue-green-eyed gaze fastening on Crystal's face. It really annoyed Darci the way that Lisa and Blythe were always so intent on being friends with Crystal they couldn't even speak to anyone else. "Who drew your name?"

"Darci did." Crystal beamed. "Isn't that great?"

"Oh-h-h," Lisa said in such a sour tone of voice Darci almost laughed. "So that's what happened." She threw Darci a sharp look as if she thought Darci had arranged the whole thing.

"Well, anyway . . ." She smiled at Crystal. "Did Blythe tell you about my sleepover?"

"Well, you see my parents have been invited . . ." Crystal explained again about her plans for that night.

"Well, in case you can come, we're going to have a really spooky video . . ." and Lisa went on about her party.

Darci thought that Lisa and Blythe weren't very nice to keep talking about their party in front of other people they weren't inviting. It did sound like a great party though. If Crystal could go, which party would she choose?

Darci looked around at the crowded room. She saw the redhead with a group of laughing girls. Surely she'd have come over to Darci by now if she was the one. "I wonder where my secret sister is," she said in a low voice to Jennifer. But Lisa overheard. "You mean you haven't found her?"

Did sort of a pleased expression cross Lisa's face?

Darci had that terrible thought again. Could it be Lisa?

"No, I haven't," Darci said stiffly. "Have you?"

"Oh, yeah," Lisa said in a superior tone. "Blythe and I found out everything." She rattled off the names of four girls in other classes. "We've done it all." She waved her hand as if she was glad she was through with it.

A group of boys went pushing past just then, and one of them was Nathan. He turned and gave Darci a thumbs-up sign. "Hi, Darci," he called out with a big grin.

"Oh, hi, Nathan," she answered. "Have you found your secret brother?"

"Oh, yeah, yeah. It's Pedro." He punched the boy ahead of him on the arm. The boy turned, rolled his eyes, and grinned. "Isn't he lucky?"

"Darci's sister hasn't turned up yet," Blythe said loudly.

"Sure is funny," Lisa said, her blue-green eyes amused.

Darci wished they wouldn't tell Nathan and everybody else about it.

"She'll probably come any minute," Crystal said reassuringly.

"Or maybe she's home sick today," Jennifer said.

"Yeah, yeah," Nathan put in. "Or she could be

80

on vacation. I bet she wishes she could come," he added, giving her a grin.

That was so nice of Nathan. Darci felt a little warm glow even after he'd left with Pedro to get cookies and punch.

"By the way, I want to ask you something." Crystal looked around at all of them. "I got a call this morning. I had some great news. I've been picked for the new TV commercial for See's candy, and I'm going to the Oakwood Hotel this afternoon for a shoot. How'd you like to come over and watch? Remember, Darci, I told you and Jennifer I might get this job."

"You got it. How fantastic!" Darci exclaimed. "I'd love to see you in action."

"Good for you." Jennifer patted Crystal's shoulder.

"I'd like to come and watch. I've never seen a TV commercial being made. Wouldn't that be great, Blythe?" Lisa's blue-green eyes shone like marbles.

"Terrific," Blythe echoed.

"And also, they may need a few walk-ons. You know, a couple of people to walk past in the background," Crystal added.

"You'd want us to be on TV?" Darci was charmed by the idea. And looking around at the others she could see the excitement on their faces, too.

"I'm ready." Lisa brushed back her blonde hair as if she were already being viewed by millions.

Suddenly Darci remembered something. "Oh, I forgot." She groaned. "I'm supposed to go shopping with my grandma this afternoon."

"Guess you'll just have to miss it," Lisa put in triumphantly. "But we'll be there, won't we, Blythe?"

"Yes, yes. You know it," Blythe agreed.

"Oh, Darci, can't you work it out with your grandma?" Crystal urged her.

"Yes, try. Do try," Jennifer begged.

Darci felt terrible. How could she miss it? "I'll see what I can do. I'll try, really I will. And, Crystal, thanks for asking us. I'll go phone my grandma right now."

Darci hurried out of the room. It was a relief anyway to get away from the party where everyone else was happily finding a secret sister or brother. She'd go to the phone booth by the office, but first she'd have to stop at her locker to get some money. She really dreaded calling her grandma though. It was going to be so hard to cancel the shopping trip with her.

She spun the knob on her locker, trying to think just how she'd say it to her grandma. How she hoped Grandma Clair wouldn't mind. Darci yanked open the door. But what was that? A sheet of yellow paper lay inside. Was it another note?

82

She swooped it up eagerly and read: " *'Darci, don't give up. You'll find out who I am soon. Your secret sister.'* "

"Well," Darci exclaimed out loud. "How weird." But she felt better, really a lot better already, and she headed for the phone booth.

10.
TV Shoot

Darci hurried up to her front door. She'd tried and tried to phone her grandma from school but the line was always busy. Since her mother was at work, it must be her grandma on the phone.

Sure enough, when she stepped into the front hall she heard her grandmother talking in low tones. Poor Grandma Clair must be missing her friends a lot. Darci was really sorry to have to break her date to go shopping this afternoon.

Darci went to the den doorway and looked in.

Grandma Clair was sitting at the desk, bent over the telephone and saying something like, "Yes, I think so. Yes, I've been missing you, too. Yes, a lot." She laughed softly. She glanced up, startled. "I must go now but I'll talk to you soon. Bye-bye." She hung up and looked at Darci. "Hello, dear. I was just talking to a friend back home." She patted her gray-brown hair and, Darci thought, looked flustered. Did she also look a little guilty? And if so, why? Was it about the decision

84

she was supposed to be considering while she was here?

"Hi, Grandma." Darci dumped her backpack and shoulder bag on her dad's big armchair. If only Mom were here today to go shopping with Grandma Clair.

"Grandma Clair," Darci burst out. "I'm really sorry. I hope you don't mind, but I can't go shopping with you this afternoon. My new friend, you know, Crystal, is being filmed at the Oakwood Hotel and she really wants me to come and watch. They might even ask some of us to be part of a crowd scene."

Grandma Clair's welcoming smile faded. Did she look disappointed? Darci tried not to pay any attention to her purse and jacket all laid out on the desk.

"Oh, really, dear? Well, of course you'll want to go. It should be interesting. How are you getting there?"

"Jennifer's mother is taking a break from her real estate office to drive us and she'll be here any minute." Darci had arranged all this with Jennifer before she left school.

"Does your mother know about this?" Grandma Clair frowned and looked worried.

"Yes, I called her from school, but she was out of the office. I left a message." The sun's rays slanted through the window and across Grandma Clair's finely wrinkled face. She would be all by

85

herself here this afternoon. Darci tried to push away these thoughts.

"How are you getting home? Will you call if you need a ride? Perhaps Rick could arrange to come for you."

"No, no, really Grandma. I'm okay." Darci felt impatient and wished Grandma Clair wouldn't ask so many questions. She heard the sound of a car approaching down the street. "That might be Jennifer now. I have to go," she said and, grabbing up her purse, she headed for the front door and quickly darted outside.

She raced across the lawn, but the car she'd heard went on down the street. And now she saw Nathan was out there in the driveway, straddling his bike. "Oh, hi, Nathan." What a shame she had to leave right now.

"Where're you going in such a hurry, Darci? Heading for a fire or something?"

Darci laughed. "No, something better. Crystal invited me to come see her make a commercial for TV." She could see in one quick glance that Nathan was actually impressed. Still, she hoped he wasn't too impressed, with Crystal anyway. Darci knew he used to like her last spring after they'd been in the dance contest together and she wondered with a twinge of sadness if he still did.

"Well, listen, Darci," Nathan spoke up, "I have something I wanted to ask you about."

But now Jennifer's van was coming down the

86

street and already she could see Jennifer leaning out the window, waving to her.

"I have to go. Sorry." Darci rushed to the curb. Whatever Nathan had to ask her would have to wait.

The van pulled up beside her and Jennifer slid the door open. Darci hopped inside and called out the window, " 'Bye, Nathan." Then she leaned toward the front seat. "Hello, Mrs. Chen. Thank you for taking us."

"I couldn't let you two miss this big event." Mrs. Chen smiled at Darci over her shoulder. "Even if it keeps Jennifer from becoming a concert pianist."

Darci knew she was joking but she also knew that Jennifer and her family took Jennifer's piano lessons and her schoolwork, too, very seriously. Jennifer was a hard worker.

Darci turned to Jennifer. "Are you ready for our big afternoon?"

"Oh, of course." Jennifer glanced out the rear window toward Nathan in the distance, still straddling his bike. She grinned at Darci. "Sorry to tear you away from Nathan."

"He was going to ask me something." Darci frowned, wondering again what it was. She looked back, too, to see Nathan still watching them.

"I'm sure he'll ask you later," Jennifer said. "You didn't find out yet who your secret sister is?" Darci could hear the sympathy in her voice.

87

"No, uh-uh. Must be some nerdy girl or maybe she really wasn't in school today."

Mrs. Chen turned on a tape of some classical music on the car radio then. For classical music it was pretty good and Darci's spirits rose. Forget the secret sister. This afternoon was going to be great. There was just one little dark worry, though. She wished she hadn't been so impatient with her grandma, wished she could have explained better why she just had to leave.

"Darci," Jennifer said. "Do you think we've got any chance of being on TV, instead of Lisa and Blythe?" Jennifer patted her hair. "At least I washed my hair last night."

Darci looked admiringly at Jennifer's dark, silky hair. "It looks great," Darci assured her. She pulled out a comb from her purse and anxiously began to fix her own hair.

Suddenly an idea hit her. "I know what! We ought to wear makeup."

"You're right," Jennifer exclaimed. "Have we got any with us? Mom, do you have any makeup in your purse?" she called toward the front seat.

"Just lipstick," Mrs. Chen said as she busily eased the car through some traffic.

Darci and Jennifer scrabbled through their purses and managed to find lip gloss, blusher, and eye shadow. "Here, I'll help you and you do me," Darci suggested. She dabbed carefully at Jennifer's face. It was a little difficult with the van's jiggling. Whenever Mrs. Chen stopped at a red light Darci hurried to put on Jennifer's eye makeup. Then Darci sat quietly while Jennifer did her.

Darci peered in a little mirror from her purse, then at Jennifer. "How great we look," she exclaimed with satisfaction. "Maybe we will be picked. You look so much older, Jennifer."

At the hotel, an old, white wooden building with green shutters, they pulled into the parking lot, then climbed out of the van and hurried toward the entrance.

"Where do we go, girls?" Mrs. Chen asked.

"Crystal said to come to the main lobby," Darci answered as they pushed through the revolving door.

"Look, there they are." Jennifer pointed excitedly toward the far end of the lobby where there were several potted green plants and a small group of people gathered in a circle. Crystal stood in the middle of them all and a man wearing tinted glasses and a black beret was busily talking to her, while two other men focused large cameras on her.

As they crossed the lobby Darci spotted Lisa and Blythe already sitting on one of the couches outside the roped-off area. Darci thought they looked disappointed when they looked up and saw her crossing the lobby with Jennifer and Mrs. Chen.

Just as they sat down someone called out, "Quiet, please," and bright floodlights were snapped on, bathing Crystal and a gray-haired man in the glow. They were starting. Darci clasped her hands together with excitement.

Now the whole scene began, just as Crystal had said it would. Crystal rushed up to the gray-haired man.

"Oh, Dad, sorry I'm late. How was your shopping?" Crystal looked wonderful, with lots of makeup on her face and her dark hair hanging in a shiny coil over one shoulder. "Did you find anything for Mom for Valentine's Day?"

Her TV father smiled fondly. "Yes, I got her the best." He held out a white box in front of him. "A big box of See's chocolates made with all fresh ingredients, nuts and creams and caramels."

It sounded so good, Darci wished she had some.

The director raised his hand then toward the cameramen and the bright lights blinked out.

Darci wanted to whisper to Jennifer but didn't think she should. And besides, in a minute Crystal and her TV dad went through the whole scene again. It seemed perfect to Darci, just perfect, and Crystal was really good. Darci knew how important this job was to her.

But now the lights were off again and the di-

90

rector was standing there, looking around the hotel lobby, and he seemed to be considering something. Then, to Darci's utter amazement, he headed across the roped-off area and came right out to where she and Jennifer and Mrs. Chen were sitting.

11.
Disaster

Darci could hardly believe it when the director stopped in front of Mrs. Chen. "We need a couple of walk-ons," he said. "Could these two girls do it?"

Darci was amazed. Mrs. Chen looked a little surprised, too. "Do you want to, girls?"

"Oh, yeah, Mom." Jennifer nudged her mother. "We'd love to do it, wouldn't we, Darci?"

"Yes, yes, that would be fabulous," Darci exclaimed and instinctively touched her cheeks. How lucky it was she and Jennifer had put on that blusher and eye shadow. Now they were all ready.

It seemed like a wonderful dream after that, as the director led them into the roped off area and over near the cameras. Could this be real? But it was, and Crystal was beaming at them.

The director explained to them then what they were to do. Then floodlights flashed on again and in a minute Crystal was rushing up to her TV dad.

At the signal from the director, Darci and Jennifer stepped forward into the warm lights and walked across the room. Darci was faintly aware of the voices continuing with the commercial. Mainly, she was busy thinking, walk straight, don't fall, hold your head up. It was like being up on an important stage with thousands of people watching. But they had to go through the scene several more times before the director called out, "All right, everybody. That's it."

Everyone began to mill around and gather up equipment and belongings. Crystal was surrounded by people, so Darci and Jennifer started to leave, following Mrs. Chen.

As they crossed the lobby, Lisa and Blythe caught up with them. "So, you got to be on television," Lisa said. "How come you were chosen?" Her blue-green eyes had a cold shine to them.

"I don't know." Darci shrugged. "I was really surprised."

"Maybe they were picked because they had so much gunk on their faces." Blythe flicked her long braid of hair over her shoulder. "All that makeup."

They'd reached the entrance by now, and before Darci could answer, Crystal came hurrying over to them. "Hi, hi," she called out. "Thanks for coming, all of you. That was really great of you to watch. And, Darci, you and Jennifer were terrific. Thanks for being walk-ons."

"It was great to have the chance," Darci said warmly. "You were terrific, too, Crystal."

"Yes, you really were fabulous," Lisa said eagerly, trying to edge in between Darci and Crystal.

"Oh, thanks, all of you." Crystal had to dash off then because the director and her mother were calling her.

There was a moment's silence after she left, then Lisa moved closer to Darci. "I suppose you know Crystal's coming to my sleepover, don't you?"

Darci stared in surprise. "Well, no, I . . . I . . ." Darci hadn't known. She was still hoping it would be the other way.

"Of course she'll come to Lisa's," Blythe said bluntly. "It'll be the best party. Besides, a bunch of the boys are going to drop by. Nathan, too, I heard."

Darci stared in dismay and couldn't think what to say. She'd hoped Nathan would come by her house. Suddenly, she remembered he'd wanted to talk to her. Was it about this?

"Are you sure?" Jennifer asked, her eyes wide and suspicious behind her glasses.

"Of course," Lisa said coolly. She glanced toward the street. "Oh, there's my mom. Come on, Blythe." The two of them headed down the steps toward a low white sports car waiting at the curb. It was parked right behind Crystal's gleaming blue Cadillac.

A whole group of people were starting down

the steps now, the director, cameraman, and others. Suddenly Darci heard someone shout, "Hey, Darci, Darci." There was the old car that belonged to Rick's friend, Chris, and hanging out of it was Chris's dog, who was yipping excitedly, and now Donny was climbing out of it and racing up the sidewalk to the hotel, jacket flapping, shoes unlaced, and hair flying. He shouted in front of everyone, "Grandma said to come get you, Darci."

Then the dog leapt out of the car and came racing up the sidewalk after him. Donny, the dog behind him, dodged into the crowd on the steps. Suddenly the dog knocked into the director, who fell to his knees.

"Oh, no!" Darci stared in horror. "Look what's happened." Should she dash over, try to help him up, say she was sorry?

"It's okay, Darci," Jennifer consoled her. "See, he's already getting up again." Crystal's mother and the cameraman were helping him to his feet. He was scowling, adjusting his beret on his head, then glaring at Donny and the dog. Donny was backing off, pulling the dog with him.

Darci groaned. She wished she could pretend she didn't know Donny, and she saw Blythe and Lisa down the sidewalk laughing loudly. And she could see that everyone was watching.

"Oh, Jennifer, I have to go."

The best thing to do was get out of here fast and take her whole troublemaking group with her.

95

"Donny, come on," she called. She rushed off down the sidewalk, wishing she could be invisible. Donny and the dog were puffing and panting right behind her now, and worse yet, she heard a ripple of laughter go through the crowd on the steps. She flung herself into the back seat of the car, the dog leaping in after her, then Donny.

"Let's get going," she exclaimed to the boys sitting up front. She shrank down in the seat, wishing she were far away from here.

What a disastrous ending to the afternoon, just when she'd been practically feeling like a TV star herself. Crystal must wish Darci hadn't even come. The director must feel that way, too.

12.
Grandma's Note

Darci felt cross and upset the next morning, even though it was Saturday and Halloween. She just couldn't get over her worry about what had happened at the Oakwood Hotel. If only the boys hadn't come to pick her up in the first place. If only Grandma Clair hadn't sent them there. Darci knew she shouldn't blame her grandma, that Grandma Clair had only been trying to help. But how did Crystal feel? She must be pretty angry about it. Darci tried to call her several times to apologize and to find out if she was coming tonight, but there was never any answer.

In the middle of the morning Darci was sitting slumped on her bed when Grandma Clair came walking into the room.

"Hi, darling, why so glum?"

"Oh, different things, Grandma." Darci sighed. She really didn't feel like talking about it.

"Well, I know you're having your party to-night." Grandma Clair cast a glance around the

97

room. Too late, Darci realized the closet door stood wide open, and several drawers were pulled out, all revealing their messy contents.

"Wouldn't this be a good time for us to clean up your room?" Grandma Clair's bright, cheery face, and the whole idea, made Darci feel grumpier than ever.

"I don't think so, Grandma." Besides, what was the use? Her friends probably wouldn't be spending much time in her bedroom tonight anyway, and probably Crystal wasn't even coming.

"But maybe a good cleanup would be just the thing. That's what I do if I'm down in the dumps."

"No, Grandma, I don't want to right now." Darci jumped up and headed for the door. "I'm supposed to be helping Donny carve a pumpkin anyway, so I'll go do that." She rushed out of the room, though she saw the cheery look fading from her grandmother's face. She knew she'd been short with her grandmother and she felt embarrassed about it, but she couldn't seem to help it.

Through the afternoon Darci still felt discouraged. But she hung black and orange streamers in the den where her sleepover would be and talked on the phone with Jennifer, all the while hoping to hear from Crystal. In the late afternoon she saw Nathan go off with a bunch of boys and she wondered what he was doing tonight. Would he really go to Lisa's party?

Then, just before supper, Darci went to the

upstairs phone to call Crystal once again, but still there was no answer. She went into her room and was brushing her hair before the mirror — even her hair seemed to stick out in all the wrong places — when she happened to notice Grandma Clair's copy of *Jane Eyre* on the dresser. There was a piece of paper stuck in it with some words and numbers which she couldn't help seeing. She bent over and read, "Flight three-four-one, ten A.M., November first."

"What?" she exclaimed out loud. She read it again and felt a chill sweep over her. That was tomorrow. Was Grandma Clair leaving? She stared up at herself in the mirror, seeing the horror in her brown eyes. Had she made Grandma Clair think it was time to go home, that they didn't want her here anymore? Had she been that mean to her grandmother? Now she felt really ashamed of all those cross feelings she'd been having. How could she have been so terrible to her own dear grandma?

Sudden tears rushed to her eyes and, grabbing a tissue and dabbing her face, she hurried out of her room and rushed down the stairs. She had to talk to her grandma. Of course she didn't want her to go. No matter whether Crystal was coming to her sleepover or not. What was having a bedroom to herself? Grandma Clair was more important.

As she hurried down the stairs, a new thought

99

flew through her mind. Should she admit she'd read her grandmother's note? Would she look like a spy, snooping through her grandmother's things? Maybe she should just see how Grandma Clair was acting, and show her grandmother how much she loved her, then try to ask questions later.

Darci hurried into the kitchen where her mother was unloading the dishwasher, and Grandma Clair was stirring something in a large mixing bowl.

"Hi, Mom. Hi, Grandma." Darci put her arms around her grandma. "What are you making?"

"Hi, dear. I'm making biscuits." Her grandmother looked up at her with a smile. Did she realize how cross Darci had felt? Was she unhappy about the canceled shopping trip?

"Ready for your party tonight?"

"Oh, uh, yes, Grandma." She had a sudden idea. "Would you like to play Scrabble with us?"

Grandma Clair smiled a little. "Why, of course. And maybe you'd like to make fudge, too?"

"Oh, yes, thanks, Grandma. That'll be great." Darci wasn't sure what her friends would really want to do, but she knew that there was no way she would hurt her grandma's feelings. Not for anything. She wondered if she should ask her about the note.

"Let's hurry up with supper," Darci's mother said then. "Dad and Donny are going trick-or-

100

treating and soon the trick-or-treaters will start coming here. And then your friends."

How many friends, Darci wondered sadly. But she couldn't bring herself to talk about it. All through supper Darci kept hoping the phone would ring and Crystal would call to say, "Of course I'm coming to your sleepover, Darci."

Darci also kept looking at her grandma but she seemed to be the same as always, talking now and then, listening to what everyone had to say. She was always nice to Donny. Donny was wearing a pirate costume and he insisted on keeping a black patch over his eye, too, while he ate.

"Hey, Donny," Rick said. "Do you have to wear that patch while you eat?"

Donny scowled with a one-eyed glare. "That's what real pirates wear."

"Well, he does look like one," Grandma Clair said pleasantly and passed him another biscuit.

"You bet," Darci's dad agreed and smiled at Grandma Clair.

Darci took a second biscuit, too, though she wasn't really very hungry, and told her grandma how delicious they were.

"I'll have to write down the recipe so you can make them," Grandma Clair said to Darci's mother.

Oh, oh, Darci thought. Did that sound as if she were about to go back home? But Grandma Clair didn't look particularly sad. In fact, her eyes were

101

sort of sparkly and she smiled often. Then Darci had another terrible thought. Maybe she was glad to be going, maybe she didn't like being Darci's roommate. That made Darci feel even worse.

Twice the phone rang but it was Chris calling Rick. They were going to a party at the high school, and Rick went off upstairs to get ready. Just then the doorbell rang.

"I'll get it." Donny leapt up from his chair and knocked over his glass of milk. The milk oozed all over the tablecloth and dripped down on the floor.

"Oh, Donny, what a mess," Darci exclaimed.

"Donny and I will clean it up," Darci's dad said. "And then we're going to take off and go trick-or-treating."

"Okay. I'll get the door." Darci jumped up. "It could be my friends." She sighed as she headed for the front hall. Donny would go and spill the milk just as her friends were about to arrive. How could her house ever look good?

But when she opened the door and saw Jennifer and Angora standing there, clutching their sleeping bags, she suddenly felt better. "Hi, hi. Happy Halloween." It was so great to have these two friends. They could have a good time tonight without Crystal, couldn't they? "Come on in," she said, and hung up their jackets and put their sleeping bags in the den.

Back in the dining room, Darci introduced her friends and pulled up chairs for them. Her dad

102

and Donny left then, Donny carrying a large orange bag for lots of treats.

As Angora sat down, Darci noticed her grandma eyeing Angora's clothes, purple and orange, long, loose, and baggy.

But Grandma Clair just smiled politely at Angora and said, "What a nice outfit you're wearing." Darci felt sure her grandmother thought Angora had on a costume, but luckily she didn't say anything more. Darci and her friends had decided not to wear costumes for tonight because they thought they were too old for that.

Angora looked pleased anyway. "Oh, thank you." She grinned at Grandma Clair. "Darci told me her grandma was visiting," she said with such enthusiasm Grandma Clair looked pleased and Darci was thankful. "It's great you're letting her have a sleepover," Angora added. She turned to Darci, "When's Crystal coming?"

"I don't know. She might be going to Lisa's." It was hard to admit that Crystal might prefer Lisa to them.

"Why, Darci, what a shame," her grandmother exclaimed. Did she exchange a look with Darci's mother?

"That's your new friend, isn't it?" Mom said.

"Yes, I guess," Darci said.

"It's too bad," Jennifer said. "We thought she'd come here."

"That's rotten, I'd say." Angora tossed her

head, making her heap of moussed-up hair wiggle precariously. "That Lisa! She's so full of bribes."

Darci's mother leaned toward Angora with a questioning face. "What do you mean, Angora?"

"Well, Lisa has her room all redecorated and she's always boasting about how she has this big room and all. And she claims that a whole bunch of boys are going to go over there tonight, too," Angora added.

Darci jumped up. She was afraid that Angora would go on about Lisa's room. Angora had a way of just saying whatever was on her mind. "Let's go spread our sleeping bags in the den and get ready anyhow. Let's forget about Lisa and all those others."

Out in the hall Angora said, "Oh, Darci, is it okay if Tony comes by for a little while?" Angora patted her medallion as if to make sure it was still there. "We'd have one boy here anyway."

"Why, of course, Angora." Lucky Angora, Darci thought, admiring how her medallion shone in the hall light. She was really sad to think Nathan might go to Lisa's.

"Do you think we should phone Crystal again?" Jennifer asked as they crossed the hall.

"I've tried so many times and she wasn't there. So, if that's the way it is . . ." Darci shrugged. It had been worth it, being friends with a TV actress and being her secret sister, but if it was over, it was over. Once again she wondered if she'd ever find out who was her secret sister.

The doorbell started ringing then. Darci and her friends took turns answering it and handing out candy bars to all the ghosts and witches and skeletons and princesses who were gathered there. Darci's mother and grandmother settled down in the living room. There was no chance for Darci to tell her mother about Grandma Clair's note, or ask her grandma what it meant.

The bell rang again. When Darci went to hand out candy bars to a couple of ghosts, she saw a car ease quietly up to the curb in front of the house. The front door of the car swung open and a girl stepped out. Darci peered through the darkness, trying to see who it was.

105

13.
Such Surprises

Darci stared at the figure of a girl crossing the front lawn. She was wearing a white jacket and she had dark hair and . . .

"It's Crystal!" she exclaimed.

"Hi, hi." Jennifer and Angora crowded behind Darci in the doorway.

Darci let out an excited little laugh and started down the front steps past the trick-or-treaters. "Crystal," she called.

"Darci, I tried to phone you, but your line's been so busy." Crystal hurried toward her. "Mom and Dad had a last minute change in plans so I don't have to go with them after all. Isn't that terrific?"

"Oh, great." Darci was half afraid to believe she was here for good. "Can you come in?"

"Of course, silly." Crystal laughed, and now Darci saw that she was clutching a sleeping bag.

"Crystal," Angora blurted out, "we thought maybe you'd gone to Lisa's."

In the light by the front door, Darci saw the

106

expression in Crystal's large, dark eyes turn serious. "You did? I'm sorry. I thought I told you I'd come to your house if I didn't have to go with my parents. Gosh, I meant to tell you, if I didn't. Is it still okay, Darci?" There was a sudden look of worry on Crystal's face.

"Oh, yes, yes." Darci felt a burst of happiness.

"We were afraid you might think it'd be more fun over at Lisa's," Angora said.

"With her new bedroom," Jennifer explained.

"Yeah, all to herself and everything," Angora added.

"Oh, no way." Crystal's even white teeth showed in a quick smile. "It's a bunch of fun here at Darci's."

Darci felt a warm glow. Crystal seemed to like it here. Darci pushed open her front door and led the girls into her house. "My grandma wants to play Scrabble with us tonight and make some fudge," she said, deciding she might as well tell them right now.

To her surprise Crystal said, "Great. I like games."

"Sure, sounds okay," Angora put in.

Just then Rick, in jeans and a bulky jacket, came bounding down the stairs, two at a time. He paused in the hallway. "What's this? A party?"

"Of course," Darci said proudly.

"Yeah? Well, I'll be back soon. I wouldn't want to miss it," he teased. " 'Bye, girls." He saluted them and stepped out the front door, closing it behind him.

"He's cute." Crystal smiled at Darci.

Darci felt pleased. "Oh, thanks." Her tall, skinny brother was pretty nice most of the time, but she hadn't realized girls would think he was cute.

"Let me hang up your jacket," Darci said, helping Crystal slip out of her white quilted jacket. It looked good with Crystal's dark hair. "Come on and meet my grandma and my mom," she said, heading toward the living room. She was eager to tell Grandma Clair how her friends wanted to play games and make candy with her. Then Grandma Clair would have to see how much she was wanted and welcome here. She'd have to realize that she shouldn't go home tomorrow.

In the living room Darci introduced Crystal. Then she just couldn't help saying, "I hope you're not leaving soon, Grandma." She couldn't stop those words from tumbling out.

A look of surprise crossed her grandmother's face and Darci's mom turned to Darci. "Of course she's not leaving, dear, not just yet. Whatever made you think of that?"

"Well, I saw a note about a plane flight," Darci confessed.

To her surprise they both laughed. "Oh, darling," her grandmother said, then turned to Darci's mother. "Shall we tell her now?"

"Well, do you mind having an audience?" Her mother glanced toward Darci's friends.

"Not a bit." Grandma Clair smiled kindly at the girls. "They'll probably be interested."

"Well, you see, your grandmother has decided to get married."

"Married?" Darci gasped.

"Yes." Her mother smiled. "To a very nice man named Edward. He's the one coming on that plane flight tomorrow."

Darci could only stare in shocked surprise. Her grandmother would be a bride? She could be so old and still get married?

"How fantastic. Fabulous," Darci heard her friends exclaiming.

But Darci didn't know what to think. Of course Grandma Clair had been alone now for a long time, ever since Grandpa died, but still, was it all right? Had she forgotten Grandpa?

She glanced toward her mother. She was smiling and looking pleased, so it must be okay. "It'll be nice for Mother," she said.

"Darci, your grandpa knew Edward, too. They were good friends," Grandma Clair said gently. "Edward's wife died last year so now we're both alone, you see."

"But Edward is quite a little bit younger." Mom went on. "So I thought she should come here to think it over first. Maybe rooming with Darci was good practice," she joked.

109

Darci suddenly realized it might have been just as hard for her grandma as it was for her to be roommates. And as she looked at her grandma she saw there was such a happy glow on her face. How pretty she looked in her green pants and blouse with her gray-brown hair all fluffed out around her face, young-looking, actually. And now she wouldn't be all alone and lonesome anymore.

"Why, Grandma, that'll be really great for you," she exclaimed.

"That's why I wanted to go shopping, to buy a new dress for the wedding," Grandma explained.

"Will Darci be a bridesmaid?" Angora asked.

Grandma Clair laughed. "I certainly hope so." She held up her hand to show a sparkling ring on her finger. "Edward gave me this and I just decided to start wearing it."

Darci and her friends gathered around Grandma Clair to examine the ring. "Oooh, it's so pretty." Jennifer giggled.

"Really beautiful," Crystal added, and they all *ooh-h-h'd* and *ah-h-h'd* some more.

"Things really do happen around here," Crystal exclaimed. "Every time I come you have so much going on."

"Yes, well, we have some more news, Darci," her mother said. "Grandma wants to buy you new wallpaper and some bedspreads, too, for your room as a thanks for letting her be your roommate."

110

Grandma Clair nodded. "Yes, we'll go look at samples when you have time," she added with a little smile.

"Oh, Mom, Grandma, do you mean it?" Darci beamed and turned to the others. "Won't that be great? I know what," she added with a laugh, "I'll have to have another sleepover to celebrate it. A room-warming party. And I hope you can all come."

Suddenly the doorbell rang and broke the spell. "Oh, maybe that's Tony," Angora exclaimed. They all went rushing to answer it.

But when they opened the door, there on the steps stood the lone figure of a girl. The girl wore a long skirt and a baggy sweater, a red-haired wig and a mask with pink cheeks. She was weird-looking. Hanging around her neck on a string was a card that she suddenly flipped over and held out toward Darci. Darci leaned forward to read the words printed on it. It said: *"Darci's Secret Sister."*

"What?" Darci exclaimed.

Jennifer burst out laughing.

Angora added in a high, excited voice, "Your secret sister, Darci. You can find out at last!"

"Who are you?" Darci demanded, astonished.

The figure didn't speak, just did a little dance step and twitched her skirt from side to side. A blue-checked sleeve slipped down beneath the cuff of her sweater.

111

"Well, I'm finding out," Darci shouted and leapt forward to snatch off the girl's mask. But the girl ducked away, whirled around, and raced off into the darkness, a flash of white and blue sneakers showing underneath her skirt.

Darci darted down the steps after her. "Stop! Wait!" she cried.

14.
Strange
Trick-or-Treater

Darci raced across her front yard and after that redheaded trick-or-treater, her secret sister. Who could she be?

But the girl was fast. She streaked off down the street under the pools of light from the street lamps.

Darci tore after her, her heart thumping. She'd had enough of this.

"Catch that girl," Darci screamed at a bunch of boys standing there on the sidewalk.

But the girl was quick and twisted out of arm's reach as a boy grabbed for her, and she showed another flash of blue and white checked sleeve under her costume. That sleeve! It was so familiar. Suddenly Darci slowed up. She'd seen that shirt before, but who was it? Who? It was so familiar. Then, suddenly, she thought she knew. She started to run faster.

"Stop, stop," she called out. "I know who you

113

are. It's you, Nathan, isn't it?" She burst out laughing.

The figure halted abruptly and turned and pulled off the mask, to reveal a grinning face. "How'd you guess, Darci?" It was Nathan, his dark eyes laughing.

"I saw your shirt." She hurried toward him. "But, Nathan, why are you all dressed up like that?" Then another idea hit her and she could hardly believe it. "Are you really my secret sister, Nathan?" She stared at him in amazement.

"Yeah. It was hard keeping it a secret," he confessed. "I had to sort of stay away from you so I wouldn't spill the beans, ya know."

"Oh," she said. She began to understand some things now. "Yes, I noticed."

"And I couldn't tell you at the school party because I wasn't supposed to have your name. Jennifer drew it and let me use it."

"Jennifer! So the two of you were in on this?" Darci was astounded. "That Jennifer! So she knew all the time." Darci paused. There was so much to think about, the funny phone call, the scratch 'n' sniff note. "You went to a lot of trouble," she said softly. She began to feel warm all over.

"Darci," he said in a low voice. "Uh, listen, I've been wanting to, uh well, to ask you something." Suddenly he hiked up his skirt and fumbled in the pocket of his jeans. "Here." He held out a medallion on a chain. "Would you wear this, Darci?"

114

Darci leaned forward to look at the sparkling gold medallion as it dangled from its chain.

"Oh, Nathan." Darci could hardly speak. She reached for the medallion and slipped the chain over her head. How it shone in the streetlight.

"It's . . . it's nice, Nathan. Thank you. I'd love to wear it." It would mean they were "going together," sort of like Grandma Clair and Edward, she thought suddenly. And she wondered if her grandma could possibly feel any happier than Darci did right now.

"Would you and Bill and maybe a couple of others like to come to my house?" she asked. "We're going to make some fudge with my grandma and play Scrabble. And guess what? My grandma's getting married."

"No kidding! Married, huh? Sure, Darci. I always like to come over to your house." He smiled at her as they started walking along together. "You always have a lot going on."

"I guess you could say that." Darci laughed. But it was true. And Darci felt proud as they headed up the street to her home, the place where things happened.

About the Author

A graduate of Smith College, Mrs. Tolles is the author of *Marrying Off Mom*, *Darci in Cabin 13* (both on the IRA Children's Choice lists), *Darci and the Dance Contest*, *Who's Reading Darci's Diary?*, *Katie's Baby-sitting Job*, *Katie for President*, and *Katie and Those Boys*.

Her books, which have sold over two million copies, were inspired by her five sons and one daughter. She and her husband, an attorney, live near Los Angeles.

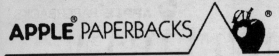